ADAM C. FRANCE

Fighting For Loose Change

A.C.F.
www.adamcfrance.com

"I turned and looked at the beast, standing tall a few yards away, shirt held above his head, his victims off to the side, licking their wounds. I took a couple steps away from the group, eyed the beast one more time, then glanced back at the kids, who stared at me in anticipation. I took two more steps toward the writhing figure, still waiting for his next challenger."

Acknowledgments

About the Author

For over two decades, Adam C. France has been an educator of the English language. As a creative writing instructor, he has been inspired by the many different minds that have graced his classroom and the many different relationships that have influenced the way he thinks about the world. In his first novel, *House on the Lake: of love and running*, he explores the life of a young man who falls in love and is confronted by racial tension in a small community. His second novel, **The World Hovering Around Me**, delves deep into the life and resiliency of a young man who becomes homeless after he reveals to his parents he is gay.

Thank You

After writing my third novel, it is clear that this process, while extremely personal, cannot be done alone. Thank you to the countless hours my sister, Christina France, has spent reading my manuscripts, taking my phone calls, and answering my texts. Your love and support are amazing. Secondly, thank you to Evie Hammer, friend and teaching colleague. Our discussions over Mexican food have meant a lot. Your comments and kind words, along with your editing prowess, have been both a help and an inspiration.

Chapter One

The sun was just peeking over the horizon. I stood by the roadside watching the money, earned somewhere in the middle of nowhere, carried over the guardrail and into the valley. My heart sank, yet a strange sense of calm washed over me. The bills continued to flutter like wounded pigeons struggling to stay aflight. Off in the distance, sirens serenaded the coming day. I waited their arrival, strangely relieved that it was almost over.

I turned and looked at the cream-colored Mustang, front smashed into the guardrail, a small trail of smoke rising from the hood. I sat against the rail as the whirring lights became visible down the road. The purring engines revved as they sped toward me with urgency. It was like watching a movie. I felt out of body, as if I were a watcher of some Hollywood feature, part of the crowd who would join in the applause as the villain was handcuffed and thrown in the back of the squad car.

They approached at breakneck speed, throwing gravel in the air as they skidded to a stop a few feet from where I stood. I covered my face with my arms as I was hit with debris. Suddenly, from behind open doors, a dozen guns pointed in my direction. I put my hands in the air and knelt on the ground. I was bombarded by multiple men, thrust to the ground, face planted in the dirt, wrists secured behind my body. I think they read me my rights, but I couldn't be sure, as everything around me was a muffled blur. The movie, with me the antagonist, was still playing in the foreground.

They lifted me to my feet, half dragged me to a waiting car, and tossed me in the back seat. The door slammed. I sat there in a daze, a feeling of relief washing over me.

Chapter Two

My house was across the street. The apartments on the other side spanned two blocks each way, darned by flaking brown paint from two decades ago. Directly in front of my house, the apartments were split by a driveway that led to a roundabout that flowed through the center of the buildings. The apartments were inhabited by all corners of the world and I would meet the world at the football-sized field behind the far side of the apartments. We would gather early in the day on the weekends or right after school during the week to play kickball or "smear the queer," a game that is now outlawed in schoolhouses and fields across the country, both for the safety of the young participants, as well as political correctness. The goal of the game was for everyone to tackle whoever had the ball—banging and smashing the poor sucker who thought they could evade the horde of kids trailing after them.

My unofficial best friend at the time was an insanely quick second grader from Vietnam named Chan. We were in the same class at Jackson Elementary and we rode the bus together every morning and afternoon. It was always our goal to end up on the same team for kickball or to join forces in any other game that required speed and quickness.

Games would start once we had enough kids on the field and

they would morph with each new person who came along until it seemed like every kid within a mile radius was running and tackling or waiting in line for their turn at the plate. Games would end at dinner time. Long days on the weekend or just a couple hours after school. Kids of all ages, Kindergarten through middle school, would be in the scrum, piling on top of the poor guy with the ball in hand. We would all emerge with dirt caked on our bodies from head to toe. And it wasn't a rare occurrence to leave with a shirt half ripped off your body, bruises on your legs and arms, or maybe even a black eye—badges of honor, each and every one. We would break for the day, smiles on our banged-up faces, slapping high fives— "Until tomorrow boys," we would say.

I was eight years old, one of the younger ones. The older guys would let us participate, but we were not given the respect the older kids got. We would rarely get the ball in the smash-down, drag-out games where physical prowess was a necessity and we would be relegated to the outfield during kickball.

It wasn't until late in third grade, spring had just started to melt away the cold winter, that my fate in our backfield battles experienced a swift change. While I was still on the younger side and I was small for my age, I was always extremely competitive and never afraid to jump in the middle of a deluge of colliding bodies. And one day, after school, a bunch of us met on the field. We didn't have a kickball or a football, so Billy, one of the eighth graders, ripped off his shirt, revealing the newly sprouted hair in his pits and a few lumps of muscles none of the other kids had developed yet. He wheeled his shirt around in the air, hooping and hollering, then tied it into a big ball of knots and started running around in circles. "Come on, fuckers," he taunted, daring the masses to challenge him and remove the

4

shirt from his clutches. We stood there, watching the madman chase himself in circles. No one stepped up.

He stopped, faced the crowd, and raised his arms above his head. "Come on you little shits. Anyone man enough to take this from me?" Two bigger kids stepped up, looked at each other, and ran full steam ahead, colliding with Billy, and sending him backward to the ground. They pounced on him and commenced to roll around on the ground, dust flying in the air, punching, grabbing, and tearing at the shirt. Primordial grunts and groans permeated the air as the three animals fought for the prize. A sudden burst and Billy emerged from the pile and stood tall, snarling, shirt in hand. His two challengers lay, huffing and puffing, on the ground. "Anyone else?" he snarled between clenched teeth, as he stood before us, muscles heaving in and out with each breath. The group stood still, a quiet buzz floating around us as words hovered softly about...

"Why don't you go?" one boy said to another.

"Not me," the reply.

"How 'bout you?" another chided.

I turned and looked at the beast, standing tall a few yards away, shirt held above his head, his victims off to the side, licking their wounds. I took a couple steps away from the group, eyed the beast one more time, then glanced back at the kids, who stared at me in anticipation. I took two more steps toward the writhing figure, still waiting for his next challenger.

"Whatcha doing runt?" the beast bellowed.

I inched closer, walking toward him slowly, looking deep into his eyes. I nodded and stood in front of him for a brief moment. A roar began to unearth itself from the crowd. "Go for it little guy," one voice laughed. Hoots, hollers, and cheers rained down in anticipation of the coming slaughter.

I reached my right fist toward Billy, imitating the glove touch I'd seen many times when my dad watched prize fights on TV. He met my hand with force, knocking it sideways. "What the fuck, little man?" I didn't flinch and began circling, keeping my eyes trained on my target. He circled with me, standing tall, smiling and laughing.

I crouched down and continued circling—and then, without warning, pounced, lowering my level and attacking him mid-thigh, just as I had practiced hundreds of times in the mat room at the local high school, my right shoulder connecting with his quad, my arms wrapping around both legs, knocking him to his butt.

I drove forward, forcing him to his back. A squeal of surprise escaped his lips, followed by a barrage of expletives and flailing arms. He wasn't trying to strike or grab me, he was trying to regain his senses. I was still on top as he thrashed one way and then the other, struggling to get off his back.

I climbed his body, letting go of his legs and allowing him to squirm to his stomach, and then to his hands and knees. I swiftly threw my legs around him, knocking him back to his stomach. The prized shirt was still in his hand as he jostled from side to side trying to buck me off. I stayed strong and controlled him with my legs. I reached and grabbed one of his arms, securing it behind his back with an armbar. He bellowed. Muted grunts escaped deep from his throat as the group surrounded us and cheered—oohs and aahs filling the air. I tightened the armbar. "Mother Fucker," he cursed. I reached my free hand and ripped the prize from his grip. The cheering crowd erupted.

I hopped off and stood up. Billy jumped to his feet and shoved two hands into my chest. I staggered back, but quickly caught my balance. The two big guys, the first two challengers, stepped in between us. "Let him alone," one of them said firmly. "He got the shirt." Billy backed off—the entire group backed off and looked at me.

"You taking challengers?" the second big guy asked.

I paused. Then shrugged.

"You gotta take challengers," he added.

I looked around and found a level spot on the field. "Okay, one at a time," I barked in my high-pitched nine-year-old voice, trying to sound tough.

"Any takers?" the big guy bellowed. "I'll be the referee." Which was funny, I thought. *What was he refereeing? There were no rules.* But, referee he became, while I stood for a moment, holding the shirt in my hand, waiting to see who stepped up. Finally, a medium-sized boy named Leroy, who was a head taller than me, shuffled forward. We squared off. He charged. I stepped aside, dove for his legs, knocking him to his back, and pinned him to the ground—next up, same result—a third ran at me with a war cry and his fate was sealed.

After a half dozen quick bouts, it was over. I still had the shirt in my hand. The group, including Billy, surrounded me.

"How you get so tough?" one of my challengers asked.

I smiled.

"How'd you get so good for such a little guy?" someone else interjected.

"We got ourselves a little bulldog," one of the big boys broke in. "It don't matter the size of the dog. They put on a show." He laughed. Chatter erupted around the circle.

I felt an arm on my shoulder. I turned my head. Chan was standing next to me, a smile on his face. "I knew there was a reason I always wanted you on my team," he said proudly. We both laughed.

The crowd started to break up as kids began to head home. I looked down at my pants covered in dirt, grass stains on the knees, and shook my head. I looked over at Chan, "I told you you should come to wrestling with me."

"I know. If only my parents would let me."

We turned and walked home through the maze of apartments. I waved at Chan as he went inside his building and I walked the block and a half back across the street to my house. As I entered the front door, my mom and dad were sitting on the living room couch reading the newspaper.

"Oh boy," my mom called out, "looks like the games got a bit messy today."

My dad chuckled, "Looks like you had fun."

"Yeah—we were playing football."

"You make the winning touchdown?"

"Of course I did, Dad," I replied with a big smile on my face.

"Why don't you wash up?" my mom said. "Dinner's almost ready."

Chapter Three

I had been going to practices twice a week for the past three years. I stepped on the mat at six years old because my parents said I was climbing the walls. In fact, my dad tells the story of my two-year-old little self walking up to an electrical socket, sticking the end of a screwdriver into the outlet, and subsequently being zapped back onto my diapered ass—only to get back up and jam it back in, unscathed. And I walked away, my smug two-year-old arrogance intact, screwdriver in hand. That's why my parents took me to my first wrestling practice.

I can still remember walking in as a novice, rolling mats out and back up at the beginning and end of practices, running around and warming up, grabbing other kids my size and throwing them down, then getting back up and taking my turn being thrust to the mat. I was enamored from the start.

I started my competitive career just a couple weeks after my first practice. While I did win one match, I got my rear end handed to me twice and sat in the stands watching the guys who threw me around, getting their hands raised as the tournament went on without me.

My resolve strengthened with every passing moment. As a little kindergartener, sitting there watching, I told myself I wouldn't let this happen again. So, I dedicated myself, as much as a six-year-old could, to getting my hand raised. And that is what happened. Over the next two years, I won numerous tournaments, defeating those who bested me before.

On the days I wasn't at practice, I was out in the neighborhood, riding my bike with Chan and the others my age, or trying to wriggle myself into the middle of the games the older boys played on the field behind the apartments across from my house.

As I entered third grade I began wrestling in tournaments a bit farther away. We traveled two hours up north. Three hours down south. And sometimes a full six hours to the east. I was climbing to the top almost every time. On the rare occasion I lost a match, my drive became that much stronger.

Halfway through my third-grade year, when the time changed and the days became longer, I found my way into the games the older boys were playing on the field behind the apartments. I don't think they even realized I was there. I just had enough strength to not get slaughtered, so I could find my way in and still have the resolve to walk home in one piece. And then came that fateful day that changed it all. Billy whirled his shirt above his head, let out a war cry or two, and challenged us to take him on.

After his first victims fell, I felt that same drive I felt sitting in the stands watching others get their hands raised. I was just nine years old, but something inside me exploded and a gush of adrenaline coursed through my body. I was urged by some internal force to slay the dragon, to take on the beast, to topple the champion. At no point, as I walked forward and eyed my prey, did I have a second thought, did any seed of doubt creep into my mind. And to me, he was just that, he was prey.

I moved forward, my catlike reflexes honed to perfection

10

for the past three years, and readied myself for the attack. As the bout ended and I stood triumphantly, shirt in hand, a new forum for my talents was taking shape. Over the next two years, my hours and days on the field were spent submitting all comers. I would square off with three to four rag-tag kids, one at a time, besting them all in quick succession.

Word spread outside our neighborhood and every once in a while an unfamiliar face would show up for his shot at The Little Demon—the nickname given me by Billy once his wounded pride was back intact. I had become, not much more than a sideshow in reality, but in our world, the world of the hidden field behind the apartments, I had become the main attraction. We still played kickball and ran around in a herd, jumping on each other and tackling the guy running around with the ball, but those games became secondary to what had now become my private little fight club.

As I entered sixth grade, things were changing in my life. The past spring and summer, I competed in two separate national tournaments, placing second in both, and my training schedule was ramping up. I was in the practice room three days a week for much of the year and my weekends were filled with competitions, and my time on the field was dwindling. Now, every time I walked onto the field it was like a microphone dropped from the sky and the refrain "Let's get ready to rumble" echoed through our neighborhood, as Billy, who was now a junior in high school, beckoned all comers.

Up until fall of my sixth-grade year, the field matches had been routine. I took my challenger down, tied him in a knot, and more or less put him out of commission in the most amicable way possible. But, in late September, on a day that was indistinguishable from any other, I crossed the street from my

11

house, walked the driveway separating the apartments, circled the roundabout, and made my way behind the apartments. As I approached the field, there was already a large gathering of kids milling about. A rumbling of incoherent voices rose from the gaggle of young bodies and, as I got closer, the crowd opened up and I saw an unfamiliar kid, a head or two taller than me, standing motionless in the middle, watching me advance.

Billy—excuse me if I have already said this—was a junior now and still hanging out on the field with us young kids—jumped into the middle and bellowed, "Say hello to The Little Demon." A silent tension overtook the crowd as if they knew something I did not.

I walked forward, cocked my head, pursed my lips, and squinted at the stranger.

"You ready little man?" Billy asked.

I paused, took a shallow breath, and stole a quick glance to my left, then right. I caught Chan's gaze. He was standing in the front of the group, quietly mouthing something at me. I looked at him with intent. "Be careful," he warned.

Up to this point, it was never more than a little backyard skirmish. I had always approached it as a fun game. And on my three-minute walk from home—through the apartments and to the field—I was looking forward to a little playtime. I knew the stakes had escalated some over the years, but while the unsanctioned bouts continued, my skills and experience had, during this time, doubled, maybe even tripled.

I shook my head and smiled at Chan. He scowled back.

I squatted down, jumped up in the air, and repeated the quick warm-up move a few times. I pulled my hoodie over my head and threw it to Chan. He caught it and I could see a tension on his face.

I shook my hands out, rolled my head to loosen my neck, and then nodded at Billy. He took his position between the two assailants—me and the guy two heads taller—raised his hand in the air, told us to fight fair, and shouted, "Fighters take your place." He paused briefly, dropped his hand, and roared, "Fight." I started circling to get the contest on its way. I wasn't sure about this guy and I kept Chan's warning in my mind.

It started like a dance—I was the lead and he followed. We circled left, then right. I took two steps forward. He backed off. He was standing straight up, knees slightly bent, his fists protecting his face. He was not as reckless as everyone else. He was content to bide his time, but he became a bit more active as we continued moving one way—then the other. He bounced occasionally from foot to foot and eyed me intently through partially clenched fists. This was new to me, so I took my time, too. Even in high-level wrestling matches, I was able to calculate my attack on someone my own size, someone who stood in virtually the same type of position as me—a stance, bent at the knees and waist. I looked him over and ran strategies through my head. *Attack slowly? Quick striking takedown? Keep my distance and wait for his first move?*

We continued in circles. The once-silent crowd began to get restless. A buzzing murmur flowed through the circled onlookers. Anticipation rose, but we continued our dance— back one way, then the other. I felt the clouds part just a bit, and a ray of sun fell upon the circle. I stood up, relaxing my legs, but continued to move. I was just out of his long reach. I could tell he didn't want to take this to the ground and this threw me a bit. It was almost an unwritten rule that the fight would end up on the grassy circle, and that was the problem, it was unwritten. There were no rules. There was nothing down on paper that told us the do's and don'ts of our makeshift cockfights. So, what was he thinking? He was not like anyone I had ever squared off against. I could tell he was a trained fighter, but what was it he was trained to do?

Fortunately, I was trained too, and not just on the mat. In my parent's plight to find something to occupy my time—and relieve me of the gallons of hyperactive energy that possessed my small body—they put me on the soccer field. They had me try basketball. They had me run track. And best of all, they enrolled me in martial arts, Kung Fu more specifically. I wasn't a martial arts expert by any means, and I wasn't going to shoot a three-pointer over his outstretched arms or run a circle around him, but I had a few tricks up my sleeve I hoped I could call upon if needed.

Our dance continued. The crowd became more restless—and from the look on my opponent's face, I was wearing down his patience, as well. I'm sure someone told him I was going to attempt a quick takedown. So, from that, I figured, if I waited just a bit longer, I might get him to make the first move.

And all of a sudden—*Kir-SMASH*—his left hand caught me directly in my right eye socket. Then, his right landed directly on my left cheekbone with a jarring *THUD*.

Instinctively, I turned my upper body to the left and brought my right palm to my right ear. My right elbow was directly in front of my face, just in time to block a third blow with my forearm. I dropped into a squat, unsure if it was by choice or pure intuition to evade any more blows. Without hesitation, I swept to my right, snagged his left leg, rose back to my feet, and lifted his leg to the sky in one smooth motion, sweeping him off his feet and onto his back. I covered him with a side mount and for the first time in my life, landed a blow with my right forearm to the side of his face.

I heard nothing, save for the hushed ahhh from the masses surrounding our battle. And I continued, not with primitive blows to his face, but back to my three days a week training as I mounted him, tied up his legs with my own, and threw a half nelson around his head with my right arm. His hands were free, so he began pelting both sides of my ribcage with unrelenting clenched fists.

I was sort of out of my element at this point and did not have a quick response to the rat-a-tat-tat of his machine gun punches, so I took a few more than I would care to remember. Fortunately, I lightened the pressure on his legs, pulled my arm from around his neck and he squirmed to his belly. As he was regaining his senses, I was able to catch him on his stomach and hold him on the ground. My hips were off to one side. I hooked his right leg with my left, elevated it just a bit, and pressured him forward with my chest. I slapped a cross-face on him from behind, grabbed his far arm, and pulled it tightly across his nose. As I tugged on his arm and held him there, I could feel his squirming slow down as he tried to figure out how to free himself.

We lay there for a few minutes—he would lay motionless for a while, fight violently trying to escape, and then lie motionless again. This repeated several times. Each time he fought, I tightened my grip. Each time he fought, the crowd wailed—"finish him off—hit him again—rip his arm off."

But I didn't. I did what I was trained to do. I wrapped my opponent up, controlled him, and did it, for the most part, with as little damage as possible.

Finally, I heard Billy above me. "Okay guys, I think this one's over." But I didn't let go. Not yet. "Okay little man, let him go."

Again, I kept him wrapped up tightly. I had never been hit in the face before. And, just like every other time obstacles came my way—getting eliminated from my first competition three years ago, losing a match at a local tournament, taking second at Nationals—I was determined to never let it happen again.

"You done?" I asked quietly of my victim. He didn't answer. I squeezed a bit harder. A muffled wheezing slowly escaped his lips as he fought the discomfort. He grunted. He took a shallow breath and blew it out—spittle flew from his lips and perched on his bicep that was tightly pulled across his face. For some reason, I felt the tags on my face swell with blood and I couldn't let go. I whispered with slow intensity in his ear. "I've got all night."

I felt a tap on my back. "Hey, let's be done." It was Chan. "You can let him go."

I took a deep breath, but paused before I released my grip, slowly got to my knees, and stood up. Chan stood beside me. My victim sat up, but didn't rise. "The Little Demon is still undefeated," Billy bellowed as he reached over and raised my hand in the air.

The crowd woke up—cheered, clapped, hollered—and then, suddenly, I was pelted by flying objects. Kids were throwing things at me. Something was hitting me and then landing on the ground at my feet. I looked around to see what they were doing and then looked down to see coins of all kinds—quarters, nickels, pennies, dimes. They were throwing spare change at me. Whatever was in their pockets was flung into the air, landing at my feet. It was akin to the offerings thrown to an ancient Greek gladiator after slaying the lion in the coliseum.

I turned to Chan. We looked at each other and shrugged.

A few minutes later some of the guys started a kickball game while a few lingered around our makeshift fight ring. I watched as my opponent got up and walked away with three other kids I hadn't seen before. A few kids walked over and patted me on the back. "Way to go Dem—O—n..." one of them chortled.

The crowd finally dispersed. Billy left, too mature for the childish game of kickball he had declared a few weeks ago. He now only came for the fight action and his role as self-appointed referee. Others joined in kickball.

"You guys gonna play?" Johnny, one of our friends since second grade, called to us from the line of kids waiting to form teams.

Chan looked over at me. Then back at Johnny. "Nah, not today." He threw his arm around my shoulder. "Let's pick up your winnings and head home." Somehow he always knew what to do. He knew today was a big deal. He knew it wasn't just another scuffle in the field behind the apartments. He knew it had a different meaning and these backyard brawls would never be what they once were.

As we squatted down, picked up as much of the loose change as we could, and stuffed our pockets full, Chan turned to me, "Love those shiners on your face," he laughed.

We made the short journey home, the pockets of both our jeans singing with the gratitude that was thrown my way after the match, our sixth-grade selves felt like men.

"Alright man," Chan said as we approached his apartment. "I'll see you on the bus tomorrow."

"Yeah—on the bus." I paused as he turned to head inside. "Hey, Chan," I yelled after him.

"What's up?" He turned and looked at me quizzically.

"Thanks."

"What for?"

17

"For being there with me?"

"Of course. I wouldn't miss it."

I watched him enter the outside door of his apartment building and then made my way home, through the apartments, past the roundabout, and across the street. When I got home, Mom was in the kitchen cooking dinner and Dad was out in the garage. I did my usual thing, headed to the bathroom and washed up for dinner. When I looked in the mirror I got my first glimpse of what two solid jabs could do. A red welt filled a good portion of my cheek under my left eye and my right eye was swollen with a reddish-purple semicircle underneath. *I'll have some explaining to do,* I thought to myself.

As I exited the bathroom, my sister walked down the hallway from her bedroom. "What's up with your face?" she laughed. "Looks like you ran into a truck."

"More like a foot," I replied.

"Must've been a big foot."

"Sure felt like it."

"And I'm sure you deserved it," she said smugly as she passed me and nudged my shoulder.

I got to my room and plopped down on my bed. The events of the past ninety minutes sat in my mind. A smile emerged on my face as I relived the battle—the control I felt as the unknown challenger, two heads taller, squirmed within my grasp. I picked up the current issue of the USA Wrestling magazine that lay beside my bed. I pawed through it looking for the dog-eared page I had already read dozens of times. The title of the article, "Young Gladiators Take the Mat at Kids Nationals."

I scrolled my finger down a row of names until I found mine. I felt happy, but not satisfied. I can still see the look of satisfaction on my opponent's face as his hand was raised.

18

Oklahoma, I thought. I tried to picture his practice room somewhere a few states away. I tried to see him running around the room warming up, wrestling live, doing sprints at the end of practice. This was an exercise I learned from my coach. "Try to think about what your opponent is doing and do a little bit more," he told us at practice a few weeks ago. And, while I may have been taking it a bit more literally than he was suggesting, that is what motivated me to outwork the guy from Oklahoma and to make sure I was the one on top of the podium next time.

* * *

Dinner that night was interesting. Neither of my parents was worried about my ability to take care of myself and make good decisions and they never really overreacted too much, even when I would come home "wounded" from battle, whether from impromptu playtime on the field behind the apartments, or a scheduled practice or match on the mat.

I remember one time, in fifth grade, I was wrestling in a close match when I busted my lip open. I got knocked in the face and bit through my bottom lip—it was gushing blood and hanging by a few strands of skin. My dad just wadded up some paper towels and had me bite down on them until the match was over. I ended up winning and taking care of the wound as best we could before my next match. Two matches later, I ended the tournament undefeated. But that night at dinner, I could see a bit more concern on both my parents' faces.

"So, are you going to let us in on what happened?" my dad said as he passed a dish of peas around the table.

"I got kicked in the face," I said matter-of-factly.

"Looks like more than one kick," my mom said.

"Yeah, probably," I smiled. "I got stuck in a pile of guys trying to tackle Billy. "It may have been two feet. I'm not sure."

"Billy's still out there playing with you guys?" Mom delved a little deeper into the situation. "Isn't he a bit old to be roughhousing with you?" she added.

"Probably," I shrugged.

"He's a junior in high school," my sister chimed in. "He's two years older than me."

I shot her a scowl.

"You watch out for yourself," my dad warned. "You could find yourself on the side of the mat with an injury."

"I'm okay. It looks worse than it is."

"I know it's fun goofing around with your friends and we don't have a problem with that. But, you just want to make sure the risks are worth it."

"Yeah, Dad," I smirked.

"Remember, you're planning on traveling to some big tournaments this year and you don't want to miss out because of something that could have been easily prevented." He looked at me, eyebrows raised, and nodded.

"I get it, Dad."

Or did I?

Chapter Four

I was on the mat warming up with my teammates. The remnants of the run-in with the fists of my latest challenger had faded to a soft discoloring under each eye. My left cheek was a tinge yellow and my right eye still had a hint of purple outlined in yellow, but the swelling was gone. We always started practice by running around the mat, doing an agility warm-up with somersaults, cartwheels, hops, sprints—and then into some low-level drills.

After warm-ups, I grabbed a partner. We pummeled for a few minutes before moving to snap and movement drills. I snapped my partner into a front headlock, pulled and moved him around as he worked to stay in good position on his feet. My job was to move him around for thirty seconds while he circled forward and controlled my elbow. We switched on and off, each taking our turn snapping and moving the other until we got a good sweat going.

Since today was a Greco focus, we worked on our backstep to arm throw. We took turns setting our hand on the other's shoulder while the other would trap the arm, step in with one foot—back step with the other—then swivel his hips, and pop with a quick snapping motion, only executing the initial part of the move, both remaining on our feet. This quick-paced warm-up drill made the movement second nature. It was almost like a dance. Once you got good at it, you could hit eight or ten quick back steps in succession, one side and then the other.

We spent the next fifteen minutes working full arm throws. The sound of bodies hitting the mat reverberated through the room. I was able to throw from both sides, but I was always best going to my left, not uncommon for a right-hander. My partner, on the other hand, had an uncanny ability to throw almost perfectly from both sides. Part of my problem was that I was so competitive I didn't give myself a chance to slow down and work on my weak side. I kept trying to keep up with my partner.

After a short break, we worked on back steps to a head and arm before breaking into groups of three for pummel matches. A pummel match consisted of two rounds. The first round was one minute of hard pummeling, trying to off-balance your partner. When the whistle blew, it was round two, a live go for two minutes.

I loved live wrestling. While my partners may best me in technique, I was almost always able to gain the upper hand when we went live. I loved the grind of live wrestling from the first day I stepped on the mat. There was something about it that felt natural to me. It wasn't about winning. It was about the struggle. It was about sweating. It was about pushing and pulling and never giving up. Sometimes it didn't matter to me if there was a takedown won or lost. My favorite thing was everything in between—grabbing, jostling for position, blocking an attack, reattacking, working my way back to good position after my partner stuffed my face into the mat. I enjoyed every aspect of it.

After we were done and we had finished with sprints and a

warm-down, I loved lying on my back and feeling the sweat drip down my neck and back and then getting up and seeing the pool of water my body had created. It was visual evidence of the work. This was the same reason I enjoyed my bouts on the field behind the apartments. While I never told anyone, I relished the welts that grew under my eyes after I was punched in the face for the first time. I loved the feeling of blocking the next punch and then hearing the thud of my opponent's body as I took him to the ground. I almost loved the field matches more than the measured bouts that started and stopped by the referee's whistle, where points were kept to determine a winner. If I didn't know any better, I might even say I was addicted to the matches on the grass, the matches in the field behind the apartments. There were no rules. There was no time limit. There was no score to determine the winner. It felt real. It felt primal.

I loved standing up and looking at the aftermath. The dirt on my clothes. My grass-stained knees. My opponent lying on the ground, stunned. And while those matches were getting fewer and farther between as wrestling took more precedence in my life, I would find my way back behind the apartments every couple of weeks to take on new challengers. Sometimes one of the kids from my neighborhood would gain the courage to step toe to toe with me. Other times a new face from blocks or even miles away would be my next victim. And the new tradition, the throwing of loose change, had now become a custom. Each time a bout was over, Chan and I would bend down and collect the shiny coins. Most of the time it would be just a couple bucks, but it was fun. It was amusing. It added mystique to the battles.

But, that day, at the end of practice early in my sixth-grade year, I realized my days in the field were limited. My coach pulled me aside and asked how I was doing. He noticed the aftermath of the off-the-mat skirmishes on my face and was concerned. And after that, I tried to stay away from the field, at least, at first.

I did manage to stay away for a few weeks. I went home after school. I went to practice three days a week. I traveled with my team to Cedar Falls, Iowa for pre-season Nationals. Yet each day I rode the bus home from school, I would be bombarded with questions about the field—about when I would be back. I would inevitably hear about a new kid who was in waiting, a mysterious brawler who was ready to take me on. But I would resist the urge until one drizzly late fall day, just a few days after I collected a silver medal at the pre-season Nationals.

I was riding my bike with Chan and rounded the corner on the far side of the apartments, stopping on the outskirts of the field. We could hear a rumble coming from the usual group of kids on the far end. We hopped off our bikes and watched. At first, from a distance, it looked like a scrum of arms and legs tackling some poor soul and piling on top of him, but then the hoard opened up and revealed a slugfest in the center. It appeared that one kid was sitting on top of another, pummeling him repeatedly, while the onlookers roared like savages.

We hopped back on our bikes and made a mad dash for the action. When we got closer, we could see that the flailing hands coming down on the young boy huddled on the ground were somewhat harmless, but were still being thrust upon him with fury and no one was coming to the aid of the victim. There was a clear absence of older kids who normally kept things under a semblance of control, so the action that was usually somewhat guarded had gotten out of hand.

We threw our bikes down and dashed toward the action. We

both reached down, grabbed a limb, and pulled the assailant off the huddled mass beneath. Just as soon as we tossed him to the ground, he was back on his feet, charging at us. He collided head-first into Chan. They toppled to the ground and began rolling from side to side, jostling for position. I hesitated for a moment, waiting to see if Chan would gain the advantage, but he ended up on bottom and was taking fists to the midsection. The crowd bellowed, egging on the aggressor.

I hopped on top of the pile, wrapped my legs around the unknown foe, threw my arms around his head, and leaned back, freeing Chan from his clutches. I held on tight as he thrashed around, flailing his arms, trying to get free. When the action tapered off, I ended up on my back with the stranger in my grasp. I held tight with both arms and legs. I stayed in control, immobilizing him, waiting for him to raise the white flag. The crowd closed in on us, a light murmur was all that was audible. Normally, Billy would end the bout with his deep voice booming above the pre-pubescent hecklers. But there was no Billy. There was no older kid around to end the fight, to pull us back to reality.

As I held tight and controlled the body on top of me, I looked around, trying to figure out how to bring this to an end. Chan was sitting on the ground to my left, a small streak of blood trailed from one nostril to his upper lip. Dozens of eyeballs looked on in anticipation. I felt tension in the body that lay in my grasp, as if it was ready to burst at any moment and I wasn't sure I could let go without putting myself in danger.

"Are you done?" I questioned firmly.

"Fuck you," he growled.

"Come on man, you need to relax," I replied.

"Fuck off," he steamed.

I looked over at Chan. He shrugged and rolled his eyes, and then, as a warning, he urged the stranger to give in. "You sure, man? You don't know what you're dealing with."

The only reply was a thrashing of arms and a muffled struggle to get free.

I took a deep breath and slipped my right forearm under his chin, coiling my arm like a constrictor around his neck. I grabbed my left bicep and placed my left hand behind his head. I had never tried to submit anyone before, but I didn't know what else to do. Luckily one of my teammates' older brothers taught us a few Jiu-Jitsu submissions when I stayed overnight at their house last summer.

I kept the lock as loose as possible and looked around the crowd. For the first time I wished Billy was there. I never realized how the older "referees" really made a difference. As I peered into the faces of the young crowd, it became real. I was the fail-safe today.

I slowly tightened my arm around his neck, pushing forward on the back of his head. He started coughing. The crowd roared.

I loosened my grip and gave him one last chance. "Are you done?"

"No fucken way," he wheezed.

So, with each exhale, and with a mind of its own, the coiled snake tightened.

"His face is turning red," someone cheered. Hoots and hollers erupted.

They didn't understand the gravity of the current predicament— as the coiled snake systematically cut off air to the victim's lungs.

I held the constrictor steady as I waited for my foe to give me some indication of surrender. And finally, as I felt his muscles relax, I released the coil and popped to my feet. I knelt down beside him, my heart pounding, hoping to see his chest move up and down. And before long, I felt relief as I heard air escaping his lips. He sat up, blinked, and shook his head slowly.

"You okay?" I asked.

He looked at me and coughed, his eyes glazed over. "Yeah—I'm fine," he gasped stubbornly.

I helped him to his feet. He looked at me cock-eyed and then dropped his head. A boy from the crowd darted out and threw his arms around the stranger. "I told you not to mess with that kid."

"What happened?" the stubborn boy asked him, shaking his head.

"All I know is he squeezed you really hard and your face turned red."

"Last thing I remember is someone jumped on me."

"I think you were the one jumping on people," the kid from the crowd said. "He was just trying to get you to stop."

I watched as they walked off. I felt an interesting sense of control in that moment, something completely different than I had felt before. And, over the next couple of years, it is that feeling of control, the feeling of complete dominance, that had me hooked, and I couldn't stay away.

I turned around to the group of kids who had cheered me on—who naively looked on as a boy's life hung in the balance. They were lining up for their normal game of kickball as if nothing had happened. The regular yelling, squabbles, and dust-ups were underway at the far end of the field, the red ball rolled to the kid standing at home plate—a swing of the foot and a mad dash for first base—next kid up.

I stood there in my own little world, feeling the satisfaction of being the savior who swooped in with my unofficial superhero moniker and pulled the bad guy off his victim and wrestled him to submission.

Finally, Chan, who was bending over picking up the loose change off the ground—gathering the prize money that had been hurled at me after my victory—woke me from my daze. "Hey, my pockets are full, you'll have to carry the rest."

I looked over, smiled, and joined Chan on the ground.

Chapter Five

It was in the dark of my room, at night when the world was fast asleep, that dreams pervaded my subconscious and urged me on. I loved battling on the mat during practice. I loved traveling to different pockets of the country to take on foes unknown. I loved the fundamental, basic, down to earth scraps on the field behind the apartments. And it was in my darkened fantasies that my desires grew as if they were thrown into a firepit each night to be annealed and shaped more precisely each time.

I would go to sleep in the solitude of my room after a hard practice or scrap in the field behind the apartments and I would relive the experience. I would dream in technicolor—in 3D—in 4K. My mind would revise—would reshape the images into a new reality—into my reality. And each time I woke I would see my dreams as clearly as the actual events, as if my dreams were the primordial ooze from which my new reality was forged. I was never confused, though. I never mistakenly thought my dreams were actually real. I knew the difference. But what I dreamt, I felt I could accomplish, and this feeling drove me further. This increased my confidence, my willingness, my desire to push myself to the limit—to improve—to step further out and challenge myself.

I also dreamt in the light of day. I continuously daydreamed about my battles on the grass. I constantly thought about how to better myself on the mat. By the end of middle school, it had become an obsession. I'm not sure how many unofficial matches I had won on the field behind the apartments by that time, but conservatively, it was dozens. I did know that I had wrestled hundreds of official matches in my eight years on the mat and I always wanted more.

It was late June, school was about over for the year and I was bound for high school in a little over two months. I had a full summer of wrestling scheduled—training, camps, Nationals. I knew these were the things I needed to do if I wanted the reality I created in my dreams to become the reality I lived in my life.

I sat on my bed the night before the last day of school. I closed my eyes and ran through images of my time on the field behind the apartments. I skipped the early days of kickball and running around trying to tackle the older kids with the football. I revisited dozens of scraps I had with kids from our neighborhood and beyond. I remembered the first real challenge, the two punches that landed square on my face. I could feel myself smile as not only the images, but the thudding sounds of fist on bone reverberated a tactile memory through my head.

I knew my time on the field behind the apartments had come to a close a few weeks ago. I felt I was getting too old and it had become a detriment to the goals in my life and, in fact, there had been no real challenge for a couple of years. While an occasional brave soul would step up and give me a bit of a challenge for a moment before I took them to the ground and finished them off, that's all it ever was. And my dad was right. I needed to weigh the risk of getting hurt. A couple of months ago, in fact, I broke the index finger on my right hand taking a guy to the grass before submitting him—which is actually not the story I told my dad. My explanation sounded good enough, "I broke it being tackled in a game of football." But even if true, that wasn't a good enough reason for missing two weeks on the mat, which was the reality. So even though I knew a few weeks ago that my time on the field behind the apartments was coming to an end, it was that night, the last night before the final day of my eighth-grade year, that I made my choice to have a singular focus.

I knew that if I wanted to accomplish the dreams that pervaded my subconscious, I had to focus solely on my training, eliminating all distractions. And those rag-tag matches on the grass had become just that. If I didn't move on from those battles, I may never gain the focus I needed to finally find the top step of the podium in anything beyond local and state competitions. It was at that moment, sitting on my bed before I allowed myself to drift off into those pervading dreams, that I made my decision and the field behind the apartments became just one of many character-defining memories in my life.

* * *

When I woke the next morning I didn't remember falling asleep and my mind felt open and free. It felt like a new day. It felt like I had a new path in life, a path that was headed straight in front of me—forward and into the future—no sidebars, no forays to the field behind the apartments. I felt totally in control. It reminded me of a Discovery Channel special I watched with my parents about the singularity. While I didn't fully understand the concept, I knew it had something to do with the growth of technology becoming out of control and irreversible and radically transforming reality as we know it.

I had the sneaking suspicion that if I didn't eliminate all extracurricular activities I would become the victim of the singularity effect. If I continued partaking in activities that did not advance me toward my goals, my reality may descend into an out-of-control, irreversible mess. But unlike humanity, unlike the current trajectory of technology in the industrialized world, I had the power to stop the irreversible spiral in my life. And that is what I did. I made the choice. I eliminated all unnecessary noise and dedicated myself to becoming the best. It was at this point that the singularity became the singular focus, anything and everything I did was designed to make me better on the mat.

Chapter Six

The next step for me was easy to figure out because if I didn't know exactly what to do I always knew that a few miles on the pavement or a dumbbell curled or pressed repeatedly was a fix for all. So that is how my singular focus began while I was waiting to make a more long-term plan.

It was a warm day. A slight breeze moved billowy clouds steadily across the blue horizon. I pulled on a T-shirt my dad recently purchased for me to commemorate one of our many out-of-state forays to a tournament unknown. I pulled on my running shoes, securing them to my feet. I grabbed my headphones from my desk and blocked out the world as I hit play on my phone and listened to a blaring guitar fill my head. I stood for a moment, letting music radiate through my body and then stepped out the door, down the steps, through our front yard, and onto the sidewalk across the street. I walked a few paces and then galloped a few more, and then hit a nice, easy jog. I allowed myself to look around and take in the sights while my body warmed up. As I felt the first indication of perspiration seep its way onto my skin, I picked up the pace. A mile in, I was running steadily. When I hit the first turn in my usual route, I pushed harder as the incline increased. I finished the three-mile loop and slowed down to a walk just a block from home. I felt somewhat like a recovering addict as my first inclination was to walk across the street to the field behind the apartments, but I fought the urge and went into my room and plopped down on my bed with a pen and my spiral notebook.

And then, I did what I always did, began by scribbling a few words on a page—Champ, Best, Takedown—along with a few rudimentary pictures to go with. This was my way of visualizing, of bringing the images in my head to life. Next, I became a scribe, putting together a plan of action—what I would do each day—my runs, my workouts, my eating habits. It was my map to success, what I thought I needed to do to be the best. I had read a few books written by or about former champions, both in my sport and others, and I took what they did and made it my own. I also remembered watching Rocky chasing a chicken, running up the steps in Philadelphia, drinking raw eggs in the early morning. I didn't have a chicken, but there were some steps at my school and I could chug eggs when I wake up in the morning—although I found this last part quite a bit more difficult than I first thought it would be.

I let the sweat run down my back as I finished my self-actualization, my plan of attack, my terms of war. I let each drop act as fuel, as it ran down the contours of my spine. Each drop added vital nutrients that refueled my body and soul and I was feeling more and more refreshed the longer I relaxed and the more words I wrote on the page.

That is how my life went for the next four years. I had a single focus that took me from that moment to whatever the next test would be. I stopped attending the local tournaments and focused on the state, regional, and national competitions that would help me become the best. I trained every day—running, lifting, mat work—even on Sunday, I would at least go for a short run.

By the time I was a junior in high school, I had won multiple age group state titles in Freestyle and Greco Roman, the Olympic styles of wrestling, and had finally found my way to the top of the podium at Fargo, the pinnacle of National tournaments in the country. My freshman and sophomore years I finished second to two different seniors at the high school state tournament. This last fact irked me to no end and drove me to work harder.

By the time spring rolled around my senior year, I had conquered my final hurdle in high school by winning two state titles. I was riding high—for the moment.

* * *

In May, I signed a Division I scholarship to a top ten program and was ready to move to the next level. Everything was on track and I knew that if I continued my trajectory nothing would stop me from achieving everything I ever wanted—an NCAA title and soon to follow, Olympic Gold.

One thing I wasn't anticipating was that my guardian angel would move away and no longer be there to keep me on track. My best friend Chan left our junior year when his Dad got a new job two hours south and I never realized that he was the one keeping me on the straight and narrow, keeping me out of trouble. As long as I was busy—running, lifting, and wrestling—I was okay. But when I had time to relax, time to hang out with friends, or time to be tempted by the field behind the apartments, it was always Chan who put his arm around my shoulders and pointed me in the right direction.

I can still remember walking across the stage in my red gown, waving to my family as I held my diploma in my left hand, and then getting on the bus with my classmates on our way to the senior party. Everything was normal. Everything was in order.

Our senior class party was forty-five minutes away. Three yellow buses were jammed with kids I had been going to school with most of my life. We were headed to the biggest water park in the state, our last night together as classmates—excitement bouncing off the walls and out the lowered windows. I was sitting next to John Dorsey. We used to be good friends in middle school until I latched onto my goals of greatness and he took a turn for the worse.

"Been a while, knucklehead" John said as he plopped his arm around my shoulder and let out a holler of excitement. "We done, my man."

I looked over and noticed a small sandwich bag on his lap, the contents a bit obscured, but I was pretty confident I knew what it was. "Yeah, we're finally done," I replied with a bit of sarcasm, not really knowing how he was able to graduate as he spent more time in the boy's bathroom or behind the stadium on the east side of campus smoking the same thing that was in that little plastic bag on his lap.

"Never got to congratulate you on the wrestling." He actually sounded sober and maybe even a bit sincere, something out of the ordinary for him, but I took it at face value.

"Thanks, man." I smiled and tried to return the compliment, "So, looks like you made it out scot-free." It came out more derisively than I wanted, but I didn't know what else to say.

"Yeah—I sure did. Never thought that would happen, huh?" He laughed and squeezed me tight, his arm still wrapped around my shoulders. I was convinced he had taken a few puffs from the contents of that bag before he got on the bus. I laughed along with him, a bit reticent, but he seemed happy, so who was I to care? "You're a bit tight, my man. You need to loosen up. We outta here. Relax and have fun." I looked at him out of the corner of my eye. He turned toward me and shook his head, "I remember when you used to beat the crap out of kids behind them apartments," he said with a slight hint of nostalgia. "You was such a badass little shit."

"That was a long time ago. I don't remember you being there."

"Man, you were so wrapped up in kicking ass you didn't see a lot of things. You remember Carrie?"

"Yeah, sure."

"You ever notice how she used to throw herself at you in eighth grade after you pounded a kid?"

"No, she didn't."

"Yeah, man. I told you. You were so wrapped up in your ass-kicking you missed a lot. You were all she could talk about for two years."

I thought back and tried to picture her among the crowd of kids in the field behind the apartments. I knew she was there, but I didn't remember her throwing herself at me. "Maybe she smiled at me once or twice, but not much more. You're crazy."

"Crazy like a fox," he said, letting out a throaty laugh. "But you missed out, man."

"Maybe so," I replied, trying to move the conversation to something else. "What are your plans?" I paused for a moment. "What are you gonna do now?"

"Plans? Not much. Going to work for my dad's construction company. Nothing like the big wrestler. You going' places... but not before you have some fun tonight." He laughed and slipped the little baggy from his lap to mine. "We're going to enjoy our last night."

I turned my head and looked at him, squinted, and said through clenched teeth, "Get—that—off—my—lap."

"Okay. Your loss." He pulled his arm from around my shoulders, took the bag, stuffed it in his pocket, and our conversation ended.

The bus pulled into the parking lot and came to a stop next to the others. I looked out the window and watched as kids I had known my whole life, file out into the night, a palpable buzz emanating from the newly ordained adults—eighteen and graduated—but ready for one more night of childhood enchantment in the waters among the stars.

I sidled to the front of the bus, hopped off the final stair, hit the ground with two feet, and joined the melee. The energy caught me by surprise and a smile emerged on my normally stoic face. The buzz of energy seemed to fill my body and I suddenly felt a sense of ease I'm not sure I had ever felt before.

"Hey ass-kicker," John's voice came from behind me. I turned. "Remember, I've got the fun in my pocket. I'm not against sharing." He smiled and bounded up a few steps, disappeared into the hive, and was swept off beyond the gates and into the chlorinated tumult.

The night moved forward. I gathered with a group of senior wrestlers. We spent the first hour running from wave pool to water slide, to the avalanche-death drop, an eighty-five-foot tall tower ride that drops you at the force of 5Gs—feared by young children and the infirm, but relished by the daredevil. We finally took a break, grabbed some food at the snack shack, and played video games.

I was standing in front of Big Buck Hunter, brown and green rifle planted against my shoulder, eyes piercing the target, our heavyweight, Paul Dent, standing next to me and towering over me by a foot, when I felt a hand on my shoulder and heard a familiar voice whisper softly in my ear, "She wants you, man. And she's got something for you." I turned. John stood directly behind me with a sly smile on his face. "We'll be in the bathroom." He winked and walked off.

I turned back to the game, hit the green button, shot the first target, and watched as wildlife creatures darted across the screen. The arcade was filled with strobes and electronic beeps and chirps, yet my head was filled with intrigue—filled with an itch, an interest, a sudden desire to find out what she had for me.

The game ended. I slapped Paul on the back. "You kicked my ass," I said.

"Of course," he boasted.

"I've got to hit the bathroom. I'll catch up with you in a bit."

"I've got a few more quarters in my pocket," he said, patting the front of his pants. "I'll school you again when you get back."

But I never did.

* * *

I made my way through the darkened arcade and walked toward the bathroom across the way. I pulled the door open and was instantly met with a pungent aroma hovering just inside. I found John and a couple other suspicious characters hiding out in the handicapped stall. Carrie was hidden in the middle of the group, blunt in hand, eyes glazed over. I knew better, but stepped in and closed the door. Without a word, Carrie held out the joint. I took it and acted like I knew what I was doing. I placed the butt between my lips and took a hit, holding it in as

I had seen done a few times on the field behind the apartments. I slowly let it out, stifling a cough, trying to act nonchalant, but not succeeding. They laughed in unison and then Carrie stepped up, wrapped her arms around me, and planted her warm lips on mine.

That's how my summer began, yet, what I didn't realize at the time, it was more than a beginning. It was a connection to what would eventually become a new life—a life that felt like it was in a dimension away from who I really was—something separate—something not me. It became what I had confronted a few years ago—it became my singularity and took me in a direction I never saw coming.

* * *

The rest of the summer was almost back to normal. When I got home from the senior party, I slept off the hangover from my first big lapse in judgment. I threw myself back into training— running in the early mornings—lifting in the afternoons— hitting the mats twice a week. Normally, I would be training for the national tournament in July, but since I had already signed a D-I scholarship, I decided to forego Nationals and prepare for college.

Without the goal of winning a national title and without my guardian angel to keep me on track, I allowed calls from John and Carrie to interrupt my training. I would go for a run and meet John a mile or so away from my house. He would drive us in his beat-up Thunderbird to pick up Carrie and a couple other guys with nothing better to do and we would park in any number of vacant lots or behind one of a few run-down buildings in town, getting high and shooting the shit. Every once in a while I would find alone time with Carrie and we would shed our clothes and do what young, hormonally driven teens do. It never crossed my mind that the singularity had taken hold of my life. So, I continued to train and interrupt my training every once in a while with drugs and fornication until the end of July, then I packed my bags and headed off for college, none-the-wiser.

Chapter Seven

I found myself, face stuffed in the mat, heart pounding, not able to get up. It was week three of the season and I had been getting my ass handed to me on a daily basis, something I wasn't used to. It was a difficult transition—from top of the mountain in high school and age group wrestling to barely keeping my head above water at the Division I college level.

I was hopeful coming in. My goal was to beat out the reigning All-American at my weight class and find my way onto the podium at nationals like I always did. But it was proving to be much more difficult than I imagined. I spent all of August acclimating to the new environment, taking part in club practices and training with a number of my new teammates in the weight room. I was holding my own and feeling confident. But I didn't anticipate how much harder it would be when facing my real competition—the All-American who was ranked 3rd in the country—who had spent the entire summer at the Olympic training center and competing overseas. I met him at a team function prior to pre-season, and didn't hook up with him on the mat until the season officially kicked off.

But now, I was face first in the mat, feeling a little hopeless, a far cry from the field behind the apartments where I dominated each and every challenger and my final two years of high school where I amassed a 63 and 1 record and captured two state titles. Every once in a while, my nemesis would grant me a reprieve when he needed better competition and allowed me to find a new partner. At that moment though, I was stuck, with no way out.

I squirmed, I struggled, I turned this way and that. It was no use. I was at his mercy. He finally let me back to my feet and we faced off.

We butted heads. We backed off. We butted heads again. He brought his forearm, with force, down upon the back of my head, snapping my chin to my chest. I reacted just in time, blocking his attack with my forehead as he lowered his level and sprung toward my legs. I circled to my left and returned the favor, my forearm tagging him in the back of the head. We kept moving, circling. I faked a shot. He sprawled back. I felt a sudden surge of confidence, battled hard, staying with his every move.

I faked a shot to my left. He lowered his level and blocked. I stayed on my knees as he stood up and I swung an outside shot to my right, snagging his leg and getting to my feet. We struggled back and forth. I held his leg high, against my body, above my right hip. I couldn't get him to the mat, but I wouldn't let go. This was the closest I had gotten to taking him down and I was determined to finish.

Suddenly, I lost my grip and he freed his leg. He took a quick shot. I lowered my level and circled to the right, reacting and reattacking. I was deep on a double leg. I lifted his feet off the ground, but when we came down he was able to regain his balance and free himself.

The deluge continued. He was in on my leg. I broke free and attacked. He shot again. I blocked and reattacked. We went back and forth in a dizzying display. He shot on my legs and drove me into the padded wall with a thud. I was stuck between his body and the wall, scrambled free, reached over and snapped his head to the mat. The whistle blew, yet we continued well after everyone in the room had stopped. All bodies were still, watching as we fought on. We scrambled through attacks and counters until we finally broke apart and looked at each other, our chests heaving in and out.

He slapped me upside the head. "That's what I've been waiting for, freshman," he said between breaths. He stuck out his fist. I met it with mine. He shook his head and smiled. "Keep it up and you might be able to take me down one day." I looked at him with a determined scowl as I worked to regain my breath and eventually cracked a sideways grin.

The whistle blew again. "Okay—guys—jog," Coach bellowed.

The end of practice was a blur. I was too proud to care what we did at that point. We jogged, we sprinted, we did push-ups, we jogged some more. At least that's what I assumed we did, anyway.

* * *

The remainder of my freshman year was tough. While I was a decent student in high school, I was now struggling academically. I felt everything I did was an uphill battle. I would write an essay and it would come back with a million red marks. I would take a math test and when I got the results it was as if I had written the answers backwards in a foreign language. My only reprieve was wrestling practice and I tried to relive that earlier experience every time I stepped on the mat.

I looked forward to walking into the wrestling room each day, so I could leave all the academic stuff behind, even if for only a short time. I would lace up my shoes and bang heads for ninety minutes and feel the stress melt away. I enjoyed throwing people down, snapping people's heads to the mat. I enjoyed taking my lumps. It was part of the give and take. Halfway through the season, I realized I would not be a starter. It would be my year to battle in the room, and in a select few tournaments, unattached, but without the pressure of winning. My initial goal was to step on the mat and battle hard, looking to improve. I did attempt to cut down a weight class, and was successful at first, but after two weeks, life was miserable and my effort, both on the mat and in class, was suffering. So I had a conversation with my coach and we decided it was best for me to redshirt, stay healthy, and learn.

Just like the summer before I entered college, I had no concrete goal in front of me other than the generic improvement I would accomplish working with older more experienced wrestlers. I was yet to realize that I needed a specific focus, a tangible goal to keep me on track. If I didn't have that one thing I was working toward, I needed the guiding arm of my best friend Chan wrapped around my shoulder and I was oblivious to his influence on my life. I never had that ability on my own, the ability to not allow little things to distract me, such as my personal fight club in the field behind the apartments or the secret dope-smoking forays and rendezvouses with Carrie that interrupted my training multiple times a week as I prepared myself for Division I wrestling.

I spent the second half of the season struggling to keep up in my classes and going to practice, shutting the rest of the world out. The poundings I doled out and the poundings I received became my medication. They numbed me to the outside world. I didn't care which side of the poundings I was on, I relished it either way. I was so used to being the center of it all, my hand always raised, walking through the hallways of my high school, the champion wrestler. I was now just another guy on campus. I was now just another wrestler in the room. I allowed that persona, or lack thereof, to take hold, and I hid within the battles on the mat. I walked in silently and engaged in the grueling, yet stimulating combat on a daily basis.

One night I looked into the mirror of my small dorm room and smiled. I had the remnants of a week's worth of practices on my face. It reminded me of coming home from the field behind the apartments and explaining to my parents that I had been kicked in the face while playing football. I always enjoyed the aftermath on my face, the black and blue under my eyes, the dried blood, the scrapes, and a number of times the stitches that came after.

I sat on my bed that night, my math book open on my lap, icing my shoulder, in a complete daze. I should have been studying for my midterm, but a movie ran through my head. I saw myself as a little guy, taking kids down twice my size on the worn grass and later being pelted by loose change. I remembered my sore right leg, throbbing as I warmed up for the finals in Fargo, my first and only national title, and then saw my hand held high by the referee in the middle of the raised mat on the floor of the stadium in the Fargodome. I circled back to present day, seeing myself lifting my training partner in the air, the returning All-American, the third-ranked wrestler in the nation, and bringing him down hard, hearing him grunt as he hit the mat. Moments later, back on our feet, his forearm slammed me in the back of the head, a jolt of energy buzzed from the top of my neck to the middle of my shoulder blades. I found myself smiling as the scenes of my life, the scenes that I loved, flowed through my memory.

The rest of the winter semester went the same way. I worked on surviving my classes and then put all my energy into daily beatings—the ones I took and the ones I gave out. When the varsity team traveled and there were few guys in the training room, I felt empty. When the team began to taper for the conference meet and then Nationals, the buzz of my medication was gone. I was using wrestling as a drug and my tolerance had risen to the point that nothing but full goes gave me the high I was seeking. My equilibrium was off. I was no longer wrestling because I loved wrestling. I was no longer wrestling because I wanted to become an All-American and eventually a national champion. I was wrestling because I wanted to hit someone upside the head—because I wanted someone to hit me upside the head.

When the season ended, I trained with our club team for a few weeks. Coach wanted me to attend U20 nationals. I wanted to want to compete, but for some reason, the draw of competition wasn't there like it used to be. I called my parents and talked to them about coming home and getting a summer job. And then I told my coach I needed a break. I packed my belongings and headed home, fully confident I would return in the fall, one year older, one year wiser, and ready to go.

My first week at home was like a time warp. I got off the plane and met my parents at baggage claim. I walked in awkward silence to the car, Mom on one side, Dad on the other. They peppered me off and on with the normal parent questions— how was the trip?—are you hungry?—you looking forward to some time off?—my answers, short and contrite, didn't mask my discomfort.

As we made our way out of the parking lot and onto the thoroughfare, my mom turned to me in the back seat, "Are you all right, son?" She had a look of concern on her face. "You're awfully quiet."

"Yeah, I'm just tired."

"Well, your bed is waiting for you. Don't feel like you have to stay up and entertain us." She smiled, reached back with her left hand, and softly touched my knee.

* * *

I woke the next morning to the sound of dishes in the kitchen. I rubbed my eyes and looked at my phone, eight-thirty. I loved to sleep in, but for the past nine months I was used to getting up early and going to class or working out and it felt strange to both still be in bed and to wake up in the bed I had slept in from elementary school through high school. I lay there for a few minutes getting my bearings in what felt like a foreign environment, one that used to feel like home, but now felt like a dream.

I sat up, reached my hands in the air, and yawned. The light was peaking through the slit between the curtains, allowing a small ray of light to fall upon the far wall. I sat on the side of the bed, pulled on a pair of sweats and a sweatshirt, and stuffed my feet into an old pair of slippers I hadn't had on my feet for over a year. I walked out into the hall and followed the smell of toast and eggs and found my mom and dad sitting at the small table in the kitchen.

"Hey, didn't think we'd see you for another couple hours," my dad said from behind a cup of coffee and a well-worn paperback. He smiled and pushed a chair out with his foot. "Take a seat. Mom made some breakfast if you're hungry."

I sat down. Still numb to the world.

"You want me to dish you up some eggs?" Mom said with a smile.

"Sure," I said with a half-hearted grin.

She stood up and walked over to the stove. "How'd you sleep?"

"I think okay."

She returned to the table and set a plate of eggs and toast in front of me. "You want milk or orange juice?"

"Orange juice sounds good."

"Your mom and I are going to run some errands in a little bit. You need anything?"

"No—don't think so."

"Okay—well—you'll have the house to yourself. Your sister's at a friend's house and won't be home until tomorrow."

I downed my breakfast and the OJ, not realizing how hungry I was. And an hour later I was lying on the couch in the family room flipping through channels in the vacant house.

I let the TV rest on some obscure golf tournament. I lay there listening to the subdued commentary and the soft, intermittent applause. I felt my blood coursing through my body. It felt as if it was in search of something—blood running in a circle from my heart, through my torso, to my feet, and then back to my heart again—a dizzying trip that continued over and over. It was as if my heart was sending my blood coursing through my body in search of some sort of stimulus. I was not used to being idle, my body craved activity, it craved motion.

I went to my room, dug through my duffle bag, and found my running shoes. I slipped them on and laced them up. I went outside, crossed the street, and walked along the sidewalk in front of the apartments. I made my way around the block, to the field behind the apartments. I saw a few kids tossing a Frisbee. They were about the age I was when I first challenged Billy and snagged the shirt from his clenched fist. I stood and watched as a few more kids joined them. Memories flashed through my head—I saw Chan and me, as clear as day, walking through the middle of the apartments, to the field, and joining in the ragtag football games that we used to play before the makeshift fight club developed. I saw Billy standing in front of the group of ragtag kids, shirt off, holding his hands in the air, taunting the crowd of onlookers. Visceral memories bombarded my mind— battles on the worn grass in the middle of a circle of cheering kids—my heart started pounding, my blood coursed through my body again, my breathing quickened. I felt an urge, a desire. I needed a hit. My body longed to be medicated. I needed the battle. I needed to exchange blows.

I pulled my headphones out of my pocket and stuffed them in my ears. I turned away from the field and started a slow jog. I ran—for how long, I'm not quite sure. I just let the music play, my feet move, and felt the energy flow through my body. I ended up a few miles away from my house at one of the vacant lots I went to with John Dorsey & Carrie last summer. No one was there. I ran a bit further, not knowing where I was going until I ended up at one of our favorite places to get high, an old Kmart that had sat empty for years, but was now a pile of rubble, equipment filling the parking lot, actively removing debris.

I looked around. Not much else had changed, but the removal of the abandoned Kmart felt strange. It felt like I had lost something I didn't know I needed. I pulled my phone from my pocket and dialed John.

It rang twice... "Holy shit," a voice answered with surprise. "You back in town?"

"Yeah. Just got back yesterday. What're you up to?"

"Shoot man, Q and I got ourselves a little place out on Fifth Street above Kelcy's Mini-mart. We're in number three. We're just hanging out. Come on by."

"Sure. I'm just by the old Kmart, what's left of it anyway. I'll be there in a few minutes."

I arrived at the beat-up cinder block building with a few small apartments above the little mini-mart that had been there since the beginning of time. I immediately knew I was at the right place when I saw a couple sketchy-looking guys hanging out on the side of the building. *Makes sense*, I thought to myself, envisioning the apartment as a dingy, sparsely furnished, one-bedroom outfit, not fit for human habitation, yet near the supply chain they needed to keep themselves in a constant haze.

I walked up a set of flaking wood stairs and found door number three. It was eerily quiet. I knocked. No answer. I pounded a second time. A minute later the door slowly opened revealing a dimly lit room. I squinted my eyes and waited for them to adjust. Q, barely recognizable under his long hair and unkempt beard sat on the couch, headphones on, eyes glued to the TV across the room.

"Yo, boy, you look good," came a voice from behind the door. I turned to see John, clad in what looked to be a week-old sweatshirt and blue jeans, headphones pulled off one ear.

"Hey, man..." I said with a bit of hesitancy. "What you guys doing?"

"Ah, we're playing Call of Duty."

"Q—get your fat ass up and say hello to the college boy here."

He paused and then lazily stood up, eyes still glued to the screen across the room. "Yeah—man—hey—how's it goin'?" He sat back down without taking his eyes off his target.

"So—how you been, big shot? Takin' the world by storm I'm guessin'?" John chided.

"I grinned. Not so much. It's a whole new ballgame. I'm still trying to figure things out?"

"Well—you're home now. Relax and join us. We're living the life here," a breathless laugh underscored the irony of his statement.

I looked at a small table in the corner of the room. A few half-smoked joints lay next to a small plastic bag and some rolling papers.

"How you guys pay for this place?"

"I know it looks like it cost a pretty penny," he let out another breathless laugh. "But we got ourselves a deal and were working construction with my uncle's company. We just finished sheet rocking a nice place up on the hill this last week."

"Sounds like you got it made," my comment coming off more sarcastically than I had hoped.

He shook his head, turned toward the table in the corner, and then looked back at me. "Don't worry man. We ain't hiding up in this dump forever. We'll move up with them rich folks on the hill one of these days. We're not just fixin' their houses. We gonna be neighbors." Nothing had changed, still, the same quick-witted smart ass who used to smoke dope in the boy's bathroom in high school. "Sit down. Take a load off. We'll be lightin' up when we're done with the game. Unless you can't wait." He punched me in the shoulder and sat down.

I squeezed in next to Q on the edge of the couch, all three of us sitting there shoulder to shoulder. I watched them spread blood and guts on the screen on the other side of the silent room, as they were locked into their own virtual world, noise-canceling headphones booming gunshots through their brains.

The game ended and the headphones came off. John stood up and walked to the corner of the room and sat in front of the half-smoked joints. "Come join me, boys. Time to have some real fun."

I hadn't smoked since I left for college and didn't really want to get back into the habit, but my body was craving the high, so I joined the two of them in an afternoon of fog and relaxation. I took a couple drags and then took my turn at Call of Duty—then I took another drag and repeated the process several times. I felt more relaxed than I had for a long time. By the end of the day, though, the high I felt from smoking wasn't fulfilling my needs. My body didn't want to float off into oblivion, my body wanted stimulation.

Around dinner time, as the joint supply was getting smaller, my mind was buzzing, even through the mist of THC that filled my body. I sat up and turned to the smoke-addicted miscreants who sat beside me in their own private stupor. "Hey, guys. This isn't working for me."

"Whatdoya mean?" Q stammered, through distant, blood-shot eyes—a look that I am sure was an almost permanent stain on his life.

"I mean, I don't want this. I don't want to sit here and smoke joints all day long. I need more."

"So, what exactly you looking for?" John asked as he leaned back, head resting on the back of the couch, eyes glazed over, fixated on a nothingness on the ceiling.

"I don't know exactly. But I know it's not this." I stood up and walked around the room. John and Q sat and watched me doing slow circles. I stopped and looked at them. "I need action. I'm so used to wrestling all the time. I'm so used to running and banging heads. I can't stand sitting around and clouding my brain with this shit."

"Umm…" John nodded. I may know of something. Let me talk to a friend of mine and I'll let you know if there's more fun to be had."

"What do you have in mind?"

"I don't know yet. I met a guy a few months ago who does some interesting things though. He has an underground betting ring for horses and some track racing. I'm sure he has some ideas—" And he left it at that.

John walked back to the table, sat down, and focused on his rolling papers and organic medication. Q lost himself in his first-person virtual world. I looked at them for a moment and then walked over to the window and peered out. The sun had moved clear across the sky since I first entered the dimly lit room—the few clouds floating in the sky reflecting a pinkish hue. I turned back to the room. Neither of the other inhabitants seemed to be aware of the world around them. They were focused on worlds that were far apart from the one I was in.

I walked over to the door, opened it, and walked out, sure the other two were oblivious to my leaving. By the time I got home, it was past nine. The porch light was on and the living room window lighted the darkened night. I walked in the front door and heard the TV playing softly on the other side of the house. I pictured my parents doing what they always did on a Saturday night, cuddled together on the end of the couch watching a movie. I went straight to my room and plopped on my bed. My head was finally clear of the haze of smoke I wrapped around it a few hours ago. The three-mile run home felt good—felt like it brought me back into reality. My blood was still pumping through my body as I lay there and felt sweat dripping down the small of my back.

After a warm shower, I felt like my self again, and drifted off into a comfortable sleep.

Chapter Eight

I already established that my parents had to find a way to wear me out, to use up all the energy that buzzed me around the house, up the walls, and off the edge of the couch on a daily basis. That's where wrestling came in. Along with shoving a screwdriver into an electrical socket as a toddler, there were many incidents, many storied exploits my parents tell about the whirlwind with which I moved.

A couple years after I triumphed with the screwdriver, I was sitting in the doctor's office after chasing a family friend around the house and getting my hand slammed in a door, the tip of my left ring finger hanging by a piece of skin. Folklore states that a week later, sitting in the back of my parents' car, I wriggled my arm out of the cast that went up my forearm. And then, soon after, I wriggled my arm out of a second cast that was, this time, above my elbow, bent at a ninety degree angle—Houdini in the making.

Not to be outdone, my four year old self, frustrated that the bathroom was occupied, walked to the end of the porch on the second floor of our old house, stark naked, and peed into a sticker bush below. Moments later my dad came running to the sound of my screams, finding me suspended in the middle of the bush below. That night I sat in a bath of hydrogen peroxide, scratches from head to toe.

Not long after, my older sister was babysitting me one night when, with my normal unbridled exuberance, I jumped from the couch to a nearby chair, lost my balance, and crash-landed into the glass coffee table, shattering the table, ripping my clothes in a number of places, blood running profusely from a number of spots on my body. By the time Mom and Dad got home, I was sitting with a box of Band-Aids plastering my right leg and arm, and toilet paper wrapped around my head, secured with masking tape. As they entered, I sat watching TV, smile plastered on my face. And this is just one of many hair-raising stories my sister tells about her exploits babysitting her little brother.

If I was not recklessly employing my yet-to-fully-develop acrobatic skills, I was climbing the tree in the backyard, building tents in the bushes behind our fence in the alley, or, once I learned to ride, speeding as fast as I could on my bike, jumping off curbs or homemade wooden ramps. I almost always had the remnants of a day's activities displayed proudly somewhere on my body. They were not always the consequence of a death-defying feat gone wrong, but more often than not, I did have scabs on my knees, bruises on my legs, and once in a while, a black eye from running into a branch in my newly built hideout in the backyard.

The battle scars I received from the bouts in what I later would call my own private fight club on the field behind the apartments, continued, and increased the war wounds I unknowingly relished. The battles, the feats of athletic prowess, were a self-administered stimulant before I could even walk. My mom recalls a time when I was lying on my back on a blanket in the middle of the living room—I couldn't have been much more than six months old—when I somehow managed to reach up and pull a hanging mobile on top of my head. She jumped up in a start and pulled it off my face only to hear a delighted squeal float joyfully from my lips. Soon after, I was crawling into every corner of the room, pulling things off the coffee table, soaking myself with the cat's water dish, and putting every movable object into my mouth.

When I was in my first year of wrestling, I remember enjoying every aspect of this newly discovered challenge. I remember looking forward to rolling the mats out at the beginning of practice, jumping on and off the crash pad in the corner of the room with the other young wrestlers as we waited for practice to begin, running and tumbling to warm-up at the start and end of practice, and everything in between. Each new move we learned was a chance to jump on my partner or for him to jump on top of me, for each of us to take turns throwing each other to the mat or tying each other into a knot in the next pinning combination shown by the coach or one of the high schoolers designated as the clinician for the moment.

When tournaments became part of the equation, I was psyched. I was now able to lace up my shoes on a Saturday and go head-to-head with other wrestlers my size and age. I didn't get my hand raised that often the first few tournaments. I was more focused on going head first into battle, oblivious to the rules and regulations of the game—oblivious to the need for some sort of tactical strategy. Quickly though, I figured a few things out. It wasn't the rules so much as the innate strategies that came with the one-on-one battle.

First off, I learned from a few failed attempts that my strategy, or more aptly, my lack of strategy, reaching for my opponent's head off the whistle, wasn't going to work. I was put quickly onto my rear end a number of times as my opponent ducked under my outstretched arms, grabbed my legs, and sent me flying backwards. But, even while I was trying to figure out how to be more successful, I was enjoying every minute of it. Each time I was sent to the mat with a thud, I felt a surge of adrenaline course through my body. I even noticed that sometimes I felt less adrenaline when I sent my opponent crashing to the mat. And later, many years later, I figured out that when I was winning, I was feeling less impact on my body and it was the impact I enjoyed most. So, over time, and pretty much subconsciously, I learned to replace the high I felt from the impact with the rush of dominating my opponent and getting my hand raised.

Coupled with a naturally high pain threshold, my need for adrenaline-based risk taking was a natural part of my chemistry. It was no wonder my parents needed to find an outlet for my energy and it was no wonder I was drawn to combative endeavors when I was young and even more as I grew older. I was addicted. I needed a high level of stimulation to satisfy my urges. I wasn't seeking a manufactured high brought on by chemicals. I needed to be clear-headed, in the moment, nothing clouding my connection with the experience. I needed a total visceral immersion. I was seeking a natural, organic buzz created by physical activity, akin to the runner's high that many marathoners describe as concentrated levels of endorphins course through their body. I didn't know it at the time, but I had an addictive personality. I had a proclivity for over indulgence, a need to fulfill a deep urge, and, ultimately, I felt like I could not resist the urges that built up within me.

Chapter Nine

I was on site at my uncle's nursery helping load big trees and bags of mulch into the back of a customer's truck. My first real job and my first chance to have my own money in my pocket. Out of the blue, John sent me a cryptic text. *Vacant lot at ten a.m. tomorrow. Got a solid lead.* I hadn't talked to John since he and Q graciously hosted me at their place with a day of violent video games and dope smoking a couple weeks ago.

I stuffed my phone back into my pocket and continued loading bags of topsoil into a wheelbarrow. The sun was high overhead, blanketing the back of my neck. I bent my knees, grabbed the handlebars, and pushed the overloaded cart across the parking lot to a dirty blue pickup and an elderly man in waiting. He waved at me to catch my attention and lowered the tailgate. I smiled and set the cart down.

I unloaded the dirt, just one among the many loads I trudged back and forth and unloaded into the back of a waiting vehicle that day. The work was tedious, yet for some reason the sweat dripping down the back of my neck, the veins bulging in my arms as I lugged heavy loads, gave me a rush. I threw twenty-pound bags of sand on my shoulders, carried them effortlessly to the parking lot, and placed them in open trunks. It was satisfying to struggle with load in hand, to run to the far corner of the lot, grab a shovel, and scoop drainage rock into buckets and truck beds. Two weeks into my first job and I felt like I was fulfilling much of my need for physical exertion by working myself to near exhaustion with a full eight hours of manual labor each day.

At four-thirty, my day ended and I headed home. I made a peanut butter and jelly sandwich, poured myself a large glass of milk, and retreated to my room. I pulled my phone from my pocket and sat on my bed. I re-read John's message. I didn't respond because something didn't sit right. I lay there for a while, peanut butter replenishing my worn-out muscles, wondering what he was planning.

*   *   *

I arrived at the vacant lot a few minutes after ten, jogging the two miles from my house to the rendezvous point. At the far end of the lot sat two rusty shipping containers that were now used by local teens for all forms of deviance. John's car was parked in the middle of the lot. A plume of smoke rose from the opposite side of the car and I didn't have to wonder what John and Q were doing to fill the time as they waited my arrival.

I jogged up behind them. The crunch of the packed gravel under my feet had to alert them of my presence, but they didn't react. They were completely engrossed in their current activity—inhaling, holding their breath, and watching white puffs emerge from their mouths and float skyward. I banged my hand on the hood. A slight reaction, but no sign of start. Slowly, John turned around and nodded his head in my direction. "Hey, man. You showed up," he said in a lazy voice.

"It took a bit of convincing, but I had a strange urge I couldn't ignore," I said jokingly.

"You mean you couldn't wait to see us," he shot me a goofy grin, brought what was left of the joint to his lips, and took a long drag. Q turned and nodded his usual silent greeting.

"So, tell me what you got us mixed up in," I interjected, changing the conversation to a more pressing matter.

"What do you mean, mixed up in?" He smiled through a cloud of smoke.

"What are you being so cryptic for? Are you hiding something?"

"No—I ain't hiding anything. There's just not much to tell. This guy I know told me about a place that pays people to fight. I mean, wrestle, fight—whatever—that's what you do, right?"

"I don't fight for money. I wrestle—on a mat—with rules."

"Whatdya call that shit you did when we were growing up?"

"That was kid's stuff. I was taking on guys who didn't know what they were doing. Who knows what'll happen in a paid fight. We don't know what we're getting into or who I would be up against."

"We haven't even checked it out yet. You gotta give it a chance."

"So what did you tell the guy, anyway?"

"Just that I know a guy who can fight." He paused for a moment. "—and that you're a college wrestler who used to smash guys when we were kids."

I shook my head and breathed a slow train of profane words under my breath.

"What's wrong, man? It's all true, isn't it?" he continued, shrugging his shoulders and throwing his hands in the air.

"It's true—sure," I replied, reluctantly. I closed my eyes again and felt my blood move through my body. I felt a craving rise. I felt a longing—a longing for the battle, for the daily grind. My interest was piqued as I imagined what this paid fight might entail. Images flashed through my mind and I could see the All-American who kept me out of the starting lineup standing in front of me. I felt the thud of an arm on the back of my head. I felt the power of my body collide into his. My heart began to beat hard within my chest. My breathing quickened. I opened my eyes. "Yeah. It's true," I concluded out loud. I was drawn into the mystery set before me. But I also heard my dad's voice in my head reminding me not to take any unnecessary chances. "You don't want to miss out because of something that could have been easily prevented," he told me on more than one occasion.

When I left college after my freshman year I was determined to return, refreshed and ready to go—refreshed and ready to make the starting lineup and stand on the podium at the national tournament. And that was a real possibility, but I had to make the right choices. I had to stay on the right path. I suddenly found myself craving the comforting arm of my best friend. I was craving the guidance of someone I didn't realize I had always relied on to keep me on the straight and narrow. I found myself looking around, searching for the guide who used to be with me all the time, but Chan had moved away more than two years ago. I pulled my phone out of my pocket and searched for his number. I clicked on his contact info and his picture popped up on the screen. I pondered for a moment. For the first time since he moved away I didn't just miss him, I felt an urgent need to call. But, just as I pointed my finger at the green button...

"So, what do you think?" A voice interrupted my thoughts. "You up for checking it out?" John seemed to have put his herbal euphoria on the back burner and looked at me with a bit of determination as if he was actually trying to motivate me to step into the ring. Q looked at me with his habitually laid-back visage and nodded his head.

I felt a tingling at the end of my fingers and rubbed my hands together. I could tell they wanted to grab someone. They wanted to grab, lift, and drop someone to the ground. All of a sudden I was no longer in control. My hands felt like they had a mind of their own—as if they were awakened by the chance to step back into the adrenaline-filled arena.

I put my phone, and the thoughts of my best friend, back in my pocket, and followed my beating heart. "Yup—might as well give it a look," I nodded and took a breath. But, even with the adrenaline coursing through my veins and my heart pounding a mile a minute in anticipation, I had an uneasy feeling as we hopped in John's car and sped away. I knew the choice I was making was wrong, but allowed the urges of my tingling fingers to take control. I wasn't sure where we were going, just the vague idea that we were headed to some guy's place where "you can make some money wrestling or fighting or something," as John put it. "Simple," Q said quietly, "kick a guy's ass and take home the winnings."

We turned onto the freeway. The sun beamed high above. Its heat fell upon us like a warning sign—as if it knew the danger that lay ahead—a forewarning of the impending peril. My senses were at their peak. All physical signs reverberated within me. The vibrations of the tires on the road shook the floor of the car, then my feet, and then traveled through my legs and hit my stomach, sending waves of butterflies flying through my body. I was a drug addict craving my next hit, knowing it was wrong, knowing I was putting my life in danger, but craving it all the same and careening toward the danger uncontrollably. I was nervous, but was also ready for my next hit, the next rush of adrenaline that would come from the anticipated battle at the end of our journey. I was ready to fulfill my craving—the undulating, gnawing craving that coursed through my being.

We came to a long dirt drive. John slowed the car and pulled in. Suddenly I was Wyatt Earp, entering the OK Corral, knowing that I shouldn't enter, but knowing I had to go. I anticipated gunfire. I anticipated dead bodies, but hoped mine would not be one of them. In reality, I didn't know what I was getting myself into as I stepped onto the path leading to an unknown battleground in the middle of nowhere to do God knows what, against God knows who. My fantasies of the Old West shootout turned dark as we walked around the side of a large, dirty, two-story, cinder block building, bars on the windows, garbage strewn about the ground.

Q put his open palms on a large rickety iron gate and pushed. The rusty hinges beckoned what was surely a warning cry. We stepped inside and looked around. The iron gate connected to an iron fence that traveled around the perimeter of what had to be at least a half acre. Browning grass and weeds flanked a circle of folding chairs and two sets of small metal bleachers that opened to a flat dirt patch maybe thirty feet in diameter. At the far end of the yard, three dogs, sullen and listless, were chained next to three weather-beaten dog houses.

We stood there silently. An unfamiliar tension washed over John's face. Q walked over and sat in a lone chair, put his hands on his knees, and took a deep breath. The lure of the cash prize gave way to reality. It was all fun and games when we were kids, scuffling around on the ground on the field behind the apartments. We had just stepped into a different world though—ominous and intimidating.

I wasn't sure what was going through their heads, but I had a clear picture of a gang of large biker dudes emerging from the back of the building, beckoning me into the middle of the dirt ring against a masked bodybuilder, clad in tattoos of skulls and naked women. My gut seized up and a knot formed in my throat. An uncontrolled sigh escaped my lips. I raised my hands in the air, interlocked my fingers, and placed them behind my head. I turned from side to side trying to control the nerves coursing through my body.

I felt a hand on my back and a faint voice followed, "Don't worry, man. Everything will be fine." John stood there, hand at the base of my back. Whatever he said, he looked as nervous and as unsure as I felt.

"What is this? What is it you signed me up for?" I said, trying to camouflage the dread I felt bubbling up.

"I'll be honest. I don't know much. I just know they have fights every weekend and I was told you can make a butt-load of money."

"That's if I'm still alive when it's over," I laughed nervously.

John eyed me sideways and shook his head. "Let's go inside and see what we can find out."

I stood still. John used his hand to nudge me forward. I looked at him. "Not sure about this, but I guess we're here."

We walked to a sliding glass door in the middle of the building and pulled. It was locked.

We knocked.

No answer.

We walked clear around to the front trying two other doors along the way, including a large faded brown entry door at the front and a double-sized metal garage door on the side. All locked.

"Well, shit," John said to the silent sky.

We went back to his car and sat, waited, and then waited some more.

"What time were we supposed to show up?" I said, breaking the tension.

"They said this afternoon," John replied, looking at his watch. "And it's after one."

"I'm guessing this is a nighttime thing. This kind of shit doesn't take place in daylight. I mean, if we're getting into what I think we're getting into."

"Yeah, but they said we got to meet them early so they can check you out."

"Shit," I said with sarcasm. "I gotta check *them* out. Who knows what kind of trouble we're getting ourselves into."

"They want to see if you have what it takes to step into the ring. You can't just get knocked out with one punch. They won't make any money off that. You need to be able to make a fight out of it."

"Knocked out?" I said with a perverted laugh. "I'm hoping that's all I'm in for."

We sat in silence for a few minutes and then a hopped-up Chevy truck roared up next to us. It idled for a moment, puffing gray smoke from its exhaust. The door opened on the far side of the truck and a large man stepped out and walked around to the front of the truck and then toward the front door of the dirty cinder block building that housed some sort of hidden secret, one that I wasn't sure I wanted to know.

He pulled out a set of jingling keys and unlocked a set of deadbolts, opened the door, and went inside, leaving the door wide open.

We looked at each other. John shrugged. "We might as well check it out," he said mischievously.

We got out of the car, my body filled with reticence. I followed the other two toward the front door. John peered in and then knocked. No answer. He stepped in and we followed him into a small anteroom. A wooden desk with a rolling chair behind and two armchairs in front sat in the center of the room. A large sign on the far wall read, Brown & Son's Delivery, in bold black letters on a dull white background.

John continued to lead us deeper into a chasm, through an interior door I felt we were not prepared to enter. My suspicions continued as the hairs on the back of my neck stood on end. He pushed the door open slightly. "Hello—anyone here?" His voice echoed into nothingness. He pushed the door wide open and we stepped into a dimly lit warehouse. There were no windows, but through the darkness I could see a large mass in the center of the room. I took my cell phone from my pocket, turned on my flashlight, and made my way slowly forward. I heard the footsteps of my cohorts following close behind.

"Okay—damn—it's what I thought," I said, my consternation continuing to build. A tattered boxing ring was encircled by what must be a couple hundred chairs. "This is where the action takes place."

The lights flicked on overhead. We jumped with a start. I could feel my heart pounding out of my chest. The quiet hum of the fluorescent bulbs reverberated off the ceiling as they woke and illuminated the room.

"One of you must be the new guy," a deep voice boomed from nowhere. We turned around to see the large man from the truck standing by the door looking at us ominously. "Which one of you is going to break some faces?"

68

I turned to John. "What the fuck'd you tell this guy?" I whispered, an edge of panic in my voice.

"Not much. Just that you've been known to bust guys up now and then." I rolled my eyes and took a deep breath.

"Come on now—don't be shy." The large man bellowed. "If you're gonna bust faces, you got to fucken take it. Which one of you's the fighter?" I looked at John and then at Q. Uncharact eristically, Q nodded at me and stepped forward. "So—you the guy?" the large man said.

"Maybe." He stood tall. "But we got to know a little more about this operation before we go any further. What are we getting ourselves into?"

"Ah—I see." He tilted his head. "You guys want the grand tour, huh?" He nodded and showed his first sign of humanity through a crooked smile and tobacco-stained teeth. "Okay, then. Let's get down to business." The three of us shared nervous glances. "This is where it all goes down." He continued. We fill the room with a bunch of badass motherfuckers who throw down a bunch of dough and then they watch a couple other badass motherfuckers rip each other apart."

"Sounds enticing," I said, trying to sound sure of myself, yet feeling the breathlessness of my voice, the lump staying steady in my throat.

"Of course it is. What's not enticing about beating the shit out of someone and walking out with a wad of cash at the end of the night?"

"What type of fighting are we talking about?" I asked with a bit more decisiveness.

"You know the type you see on TV? The shit that takes place in an Octagon?" We stood quiet, feeling the rhetorical nature of the questions. He smiled, walked over to the ring and pointed to the center. "Well, this ain't that."

The bottom dropped out of my stomach. I felt a cavern of fear expand in my gut—a black hole that enveloped all life, all positive emotion. Yet, the tingling sensation reappeared at my fingertips. The fear I felt deep in my loins began to expand and flow through my body and I felt a buzz of adrenaline. I could feel my face flush. I started rocking back and forth as I felt the need to move.

"So, what is it then?" I asked, in a strong voice that contrasted my earlier meek demeanor.

"What is it?" The large man spat the question back at me. "It's a rush, that's what it is." I nodded my head in reply. "So, are you my guy?" He said, scowling at me. "Are you the fighter?"

I took a couple steps forward and held my head high. "Yeah—I'm him."

"Let's get a look at you." He stepped forward, grabbed my wrist with one hand and squeezed my bicep with the other. He dropped my arm and did a three-sixty around me, patting my shoulders and my stomach as he looked me up and down. "Kinda small... but solid," he grunted.

"Solid, for sure," John interjected. "He packs a lot into that body."

"Okay." The large man nodded. "So let's get down to business." He motioned us over to the seats surrounding the ring. We sat down and he looked me over more intently. "You're my investment. If you step in the ring you are representing me. No one can step in the ring unless they have backing."

"What do you mean by backing?" I inquired.

"Someone has to vouch for you and put up your end of the purse. And if things work out, that will be me. You put up your body. I put up the money."

"What do I get out of this?"

"You get the chance to kick someone's ass. That's what you get out of it. Unless you are unlucky enough to get your ass kicked."

"I mean, what's my cut?"

"You win, you get ten percent. You get knocked out quickly, you get nothing. But if it is a good fight, you'll walk away with a little cash in hand."

"What's a normal take?" John asked.

"The purse can be anywhere from a few thousand to ten to twenty thousand. So you can take home quite a bit."

I looked at him and mulled the situation over in my head for a moment. "Tell me how the fights work?"

"There's usually three to four fights a night. You'll get one, maybe two if you can handle it. Most the time they're pre-planned, sometimes not. Sometimes they change at the last minute. We try to make it a good fight. We make more money that way. We don't stick a greenhorn with our top money-maker right off. That wouldn't do anyone any good. So if you accept the challenge we'll put you with someone that's not had too many fights. We have to have a way of evaluating your prospects. That means you'll probably be first up."

"Okay—I get that. What are the rules? What's the length of the bouts?"

"There's a general guideline—ten minutes unless it ends sooner. Or it can go longer if it's a good even match or we need to pull in more money. It's straight time, unless we need to take a break to drum up bets or give a guy a short breather to liven up the match. We have had some matches come close to half an hour. But most guys can't last that long, even if they're beating the tar out of the other guy."

My juices were flowing, but I felt as if my guardian angel was whispering in my ear, maybe the voice of my best-friend-moved-away, was trying to get my attention. I stepped away from the quiet warnings, ignoring them the best I could. "There's got to be some actual rules, though, right?"

"Yeah—we got some rules."

"Well, what are they? I can't step into the ring without knowing what the other guy can throw at me."

"No weapons. No striking the jewels. And no biting. That's about it."

"What about tapping out?"

"You can tap out. But don't expect the ref to jump in too quickly. I've seen a guy pass out because the ref let it play out. I've also seen some dislocated joints—you got to be prepared for this."

"Is there medical on site?"

"Yeah—we ain't never had anyone die, at least not here," he showed his tobacco-stained teeth again. "Don't worry about that. We had a doc jump in to help a guy start breathing once. Can't guarantee your survival, but we do our best to make that happen. But, it's up to you to go to the hospital if you need it. We'll slow the bleeding, but we won't sew you up. And we won't check for concussions. We're not here to do much more than make money. We're not heathens, but we ain't saints either."

I turned to John. He shrugged and widened his eyes. I could tell this was more real than he had initially thought—much more dangerous. "Your choice," he said in a halting whisper.

I stood up. "Do I have any guarantees?"

"Guarantees?" He paused for emphasis. "Win, you make money. Lose, you may make money. Lose bad and you make nothing and you're out on your ass. It's plain and simple."

"Give me a moment." I took John and Q over to the side. "I want to try this. I—I want to do this. But I need you guys in my corner. I need you guys to have my back—to step in and keep me safe. You need to be my team. I'll do the fighting, but you need to be with me every step of the way."

"Fuck—I'm with you," Q said in a quiet, stern voice.

"We got you, man—we're with you," John assured me.

I'm not sure why I trusted them, the two guys who spent a large portion of their days hopped up on cannabis lost in their virtual worlds, but I couldn't help myself. I looked at them and nodded. "Okay, then. I'll give it a shot." I turned to the large man, "I'll do it."

The large man returned a sinister glare, closed his eyes for a moment, and laughed in a low gravelly whisper.

"What's next? When's the fight?"

"Tonight—fights start around eleven." He paused for a moment. "But the locations move around. No one knows the exact location until a few hours before the fight." He looked over his shoulder at the dimly lit, vacant warehouse as if to make sure no one was listening. "Meet me in the alley behind the yard at eight. I'll know by then. You guys can follow me."

The tingling that had been ever-present in my fingers slowly made its way to my arms and then filled my entire body. "Yeah, we'll be here," I said, nodding my head.

We started toward the door. "And lastly," the large man's voice boomed. We stopped, but didn't turn around. "You don't sign on the dotted line, but you show up. You don't back out on the deal or you have consequences. You understand?" I felt his eyes boring a hole in the back of our heads. "People got money riding on you now."

A slight shiver ran up my spine as we walked out silently and got in the car. My heart rate slowed as we sat there, but I could feel it thump deliberately in my chest. I felt my shirt moving with every thud—bump-BUMP-bump-BUMP-bump-BUMP. An audible sigh filled the car as the three of us let out our pent-up anxiety through gaping mouths. I leaned my head back on the headrest and closed my eyes.

We sat there for what seemed like a few minutes, but I looked down at my phone and almost forty-five minutes had passed. Not a word was said as we sat, stewing, each in our own emotions. I'm not sure if I dozed off or fell into a stupor, but time was moving forward and I had to get my bearings as the large man's last words ran through my head, "People got money riding on you now."

I wasn't at all certain about what to do next, so I tried to clear my head. I let my mind drift off into another world, absent of everything but my own thoughts, my own images. I saw myself running on the road, putting in the miles. I saw myself popping off the mat after being struck in the back of the head in the middle of a long practice. I felt myself lifting and taking my opponent to the mat like I'd done hundreds of times. I remember looking in the mirror countless times after practices and matches and relishing in the aftermath—fat lips, black eyes, dried blood.

I slowly brought my mind back to reality. Sitting in the back seat of John's beat-up car, I started devising a plan. *What am I trained to do? What can I expect my opponent to do? What do I need to add to my arsenal?* I relaxed in the back seat for another thirty minutes and put together what I thought was a good plan—not a plan of attack, per se, but a plan of approach. I had been trained to walk into each venue I stepped into and figure out the lay of the land. I had to make sure I knew everything—from the bathrooms to the warm-up area, to the placement of the mats—or in this case, the ring. I knew how to prepare myself mentally for battle, and since this was going to be an environment I had never experienced before, I knew I had to take extra precaution.

"You guys ready?" I said suddenly. "It's almost four o'clock." They both turned around a bit quizzically, trying to figure out what they needed to be ready for. "I need to fuel my muscles if I'm going to smash faces tonight," I growled brashly.

"Oh yeah," John retorted, as life finally began to awaken in the car. "What's The Little Demon want for dinner?" he added with a flair. A shot of nostalgia pierced my body as the long-since-uttered nickname I earned on the field behind the apartments once more became my beckoning call.

Chapter Ten

Eight o'clock approached. My belly was full of pasta. I could feel the carbs fueling my body. A six pack of yellow Gatorade and a few protein bars sat next to me in a bag on the seat. The car rumbled slowly around to the back alley of the dirty cinder block building where our encounter with the large man took place. We rolled slowly into the dank byway between old warehouses and came to a stop. I was more relaxed than a few hours ago, yet I sensed an almost audible stream of blood flowing through my body. I couldn't tell if I was more attuned to my inner self, sitting there as the sky morphed from pale blue to a darker, more sinister gray, or if my nerves were playing tricks on me.

Soon, the hopped-up Chevy from earlier in the day roared up alongside us and came to a stop. The man in the driver's seat nodded to John and moved ahead. John pressed his foot on the gas and followed with no clue where we were going or how long it would take. We watched as the truck pulled out of the alley and turned left. "Here we go boys," John's voice danced with nervous excitement in the silent car as his attempt at relieving the tension fell flat.

We sped forward for a short distance and then we followed the truck left, then right, then left again, as if we were a mouse searching for cheese in a maze. One block east, two blocks south, a few more blocks east, and then I was all turned around as we pulled onto the freeway and cruised behind the large man, his driver, and his hopped-up Chevy.

Almost an hour later, we slowed down, merged right, and pulled off the freeway toward what looked like an industrial offshoot of a nearby town. Again we were in the maze, turning one way and then the next. We finally came to a stop in a parking lot behind a dark, nondescript building. I squinted my eyes and tried to see what was around us. The large man got out of the hopped-up truck and approached our car. John rolled down his window. "You guys wait here," the large man barked. John nodded and rolled up the window. We watched as the large man and his driver disappeared into the darkness. A minute later, a light appeared at the end of the dark building as a door opened and the two men walked in. The door shut behind them.

John turned around and looked at me, "How you doing back there?" If I didn't know him any better I might have said he was conveying an actual feeling of concern.

"Good—I think." I smiled awkwardly. "Just trying to keep my nerves in check."

We sat quietly.

"This is intense, man." He let out a crooked laugh that rose through the roof of the car. "I feel like we're in a movie—woo," he yelped.

Q slugged him in the shoulder and shot him a sarcastic glance. "Don't worry about this guy," Q said to me in an irritated whisper, and then looked back at John, shaking his head. "No matter how screwed up he seems, we got your back," Q assured me.

"Yeah, thanks," I said, struggling to sound confident. "—and stay close," I said soberly as I craned my neck and peered through the front windshield. "I have no idea what's going to happen," I added, looking for sounds to fill the car and alleviate the anxiety. Q held up a silent fist in solidarity.

A few minutes after ten the parking lot started to fill up. People got out of cars and trucks and made their way to the same door at the end of the building. It opened and closed over and over as people made their way inside. There must have been at least a couple hundred people there by the time the large man's driver came out and told us to follow him in. "Listen to me, guys," the driver said as he led us toward the building. "Keep quiet and keep your eyes to yourself. "This is a rough crowd. They don't know who you are yet and it's best to keep it that way."

We did as we were told and followed him through the parking lot and then the door at the end of the building. The lights were bright in the center of the room, but dimmed over the crowd, and a loud rumbling of incoherent voices filled the wide open space. A raised platform sat at the center of the room circled by hundreds of folding chairs. People were gathered in groups in two separate corners of the room, presumably wagering on the night's action.

I quickly began my pre-match preparations, taking in the sights and sounds of the unfamiliar environs. I turned my head to one side and then to the other, taking mental pictures of my surroundings. It was a dismal sight—a grotesque mash of cigarette smoke, marijuana, dirty faces, and crumbling lives. The ring at center was bound by sagging ropes and encircled by metal chairs that spiraled out and around in uneven lines. The room was cold, but an odd warmth radiated around me. Nervous energy coursed through my body and I could feel sweat forming at the base of my back.

The driver led us along the edge of the room to the far side and into a small cell with a metal door that creaked at the hinges. "You'll stay here until your fight. Oscar will come and give you the details." I was assuming Oscar was the large man, the man who we met earlier in the day and then followed to the dark reaches of the city. The driver walked out. The door creaked and then boomed and echoed off the walls of the small cell. We looked at each other and then around the room—toilet and sink at one end, which, from the look, hadn't been used or cleaned for a long time—a bench and two metal chairs sat against the opposite wall. It felt like we had been locked in solitary. Stale, musty air hovered just below the ceiling while the din of the crowd fought to make its way through the door.

I sat down on the bench. It had been a long day. Fortunately, I had a short nap in the back of John's car after dinner. Now, I had to find a way to wake my body and rid my legs of the day's nervous activity. I closed my eyes and took a couple deep breaths. I wasn't sure how long we would be stuck in our cell, so I hastened my warm-up.

I stood up and began bouncing from foot to foot. I rolled my head and shoulders around in circles. I squatted down and jumped up several times, making sure not to bang into the low beams overhead. I jogged in a small circle around the tiny room for several minutes, hopping and skipping periodically to get the blood pumping. I felt sweat on my brow and accumulating on my lower back. John and Q sat and watched as if they were in their normal daze.

I pranced around the room, my body warming, my muscles loosening. I squatted down into my stance and shuffled around, repeating warm-up drills that had been ingrained in me for years. I had watched enough MMA on TV and attended a couple of low-level bouts at the casino by the college my freshman year, so I knew much of what I was used to doing—moving in a low stance, traditional sprawls to block opponent's shots—were going to be of little or no use. I figured I would have to block and take a few punches, legs bent, hands protecting my face. I would probably have to throw a few punches of my own, something that was foreign to me. I knew I should keep my distance at the beginning and get a feel for my opponent and to stay out of the reach of a flying kick or quick fist to the face. Fortunately, along with a few simple submissions taught to me by the big brother of a friend when I was younger and some waning techniques I'd acquired during Kung Fu classes during elementary school, I felt I could move and block punches well enough—at least as long as the large man stuck to his word and my initial opponent wasn't a world beater. I stopped moving, stood for a moment, and then sat on the bench.

"You look ready," John said. "I've never seen you warm-up for a fight. I know I wouldn't want to mess with you." Q scrunched his mouth into a reverse smile and nodded in agreement.

I stood up and paced the small confines of our room. I bounced up and down and threw a few punches into the air. It felt strange, but I threw a few more for good measure. I paced back and forth. I bobbed up and down on my toes. I paced—bobbed—threw punches—

The door opened and the large man walked in. "Haha—you warm, my man?" I looked at him—no reply. "Okay." He cleared his throat. "The first fight is starting now. You're up next. Guy's had a couple fights—but nothing big. He's a bit taller than you and likes to stay on his feet. I hear he has some okay submissions from his guard, but nothing special. The pot's gonna be a bit light tonight because nobody knows you. But if you give us a good show, that'll change soon. If the fight gets around five minutes and people are showing interest, they may stop it for a couple minutes to drum up bets." He shook his head. "You do you, man." He paused. "I don't know what that is, but it's showtime, so just do what you're used to doing. I put a couple thousand on you in good faith 'cause your friend here hyped you up." He lifted his chin toward John and then added, "When I come back, you two follow us out to the ring. There'll be a couple seats for you there." He turned and left, and the closing door reverberated around the cell.

A few minutes later, the door opened and I followed the large man into the dimly lit warehouse and through the murmur of the crowd. I tried to stay focused, but couldn't help sneaking a look around. It was standing room only, with a circle of rowdy onlookers on their feet behind the chairs that enclosed the ring. I felt a hand on my shoulder as John followed close behind on my right, Q on my left. John patted me twice and gave a hoot that was lost in the noise that filled every corner of the warehouse. "You got this man," he shouted. And that's the last thing I heard before stepping up and then bending over and slipping between the ropes and onto the dirt-stained canvas, under the lights that glowed in the center of the room.

I looked around. My opponent was not there. A muffled voice came over a PA system, "Next up we got a new fighter that goes by the name of "The Little Demon." I shook my head and wondered when John had found the time to tell them my nickname. "He is popping his cherry tonight. Who has the balls to put money on the newcomer?" I hopped up and down and kept my sweat going. I paced back and forth in my corner. "Come on, lady luck may be on your side. Take your chance on taking home a piece of the pot." The announcer kept his tongue wagging, working the crowd, and then stopped for a moment. The crowd bubbled with excitement. "Here we go, ladies and dirtbags," the announcer's voice reached its crescendo. "We got our returning champion approaching."

My head popped up. My heart pounded. I was suddenly on alert. "What the fuck?" I said between clenched teeth. "Returning champion?" I quickly realized I had been taken in. Everything the large man had told us was a lie. I was a piece of meat being thrown to the slaughter. I was an expendable money maker. If I got my ass handed to me they would make money and people would enjoy watching blood spew from my face. If I happened to win, they would make even more money. I turned around and looked at John and then at Q. They both had a look of disbelief on their faces. "Fuck man—be ready," John mouthed with urgency.

I turned back just in time to see a muscle-bound body make its way into the ring. He looked strong, but dirty, and clearly he didn't have the high-level training I had. I could see that from his awkward movements as he danced on his side of the ring. I have been training my entire life, following a strict routine, molded by coaches with years of experience behind them. But I had been trained for a different arena. I figured he had been trained by the streets. He knew a hard life. A few punches or a couple hard takedowns wouldn't faze him. I could tell he had been through numerous fights. His face showed wear and tear. His nose was crooked. He had a large scar above his left eye.

I assumed this fight would not stop with the ring of the bell or a tap out. To be honest, as my stomach rose in my throat and my heart beat out of my chest, I didn't know how this fight would end. I suddenly felt I was going to spew uncontrollably, so I took a couple deep breaths and hopped up and down. *This might be the end*, I thought—*was I going to be maimed—was I going to be killed*—"fuck—mother fucker," I said under my breath. *How in the hell did I let myself get into this?* I felt like I was standing on the edge of a cliff, waiting to be pushed to my death into the rocks and water below, the large man standing with a fist full of hundreds, laughing behind me.

I heard nothing. The sounds around me became a muffled smog. A hand pushed me from behind, into the center of the ring until I stood toe to toe with my opponent who was a few inches taller. But, as we stood staring into each other's eyes, I noticed he was nothing special. I had been here before. I had faced off with many of the nation's best wrestlers—national champions, All-Americans, trained by the best, ready for war.

I took a deep breath and bounced lightly from foot to foot. I sucked in the air around me and held it for a moment—and then let it out. I felt a tug on my shoulder and I backed off a few steps toward my corner before a loud whistle beckoned us to begin. I moved forward two steps and bounced up and down, hands in front of my face. He moved with haste to the center of the ring and then circled to his left, approaching me with a determined calm.

I followed his lead, bouncing away from him—and the dance began. We went left a few paces, then right, then left, then right again. He feigned a few quick punches. I stayed within myself, eyes glued on the man in front of me. He lunged forward quickly and threw a combination toward my head. I pulled my hands close to my face, circled back, and out of reach.

He threw a quick low kick, making contact with my right shin. I stumbled slightly. As I regained my balance, he threw a left-right combination, each catching me squarely on opposite

83

cheeks. A flash of light blinded my vision. I pulled my hands to my face and felt repeated thuds in my stomach. I moved backward and bounced off the loose ropes. He came forward and threw continued blows into my forearms that guarded the blood leaking from a cut under my right eye. I felt a slight break in his attack and shuffled to my right—blood continued to ooze down my face. My instinct was to drop and dive at his legs, but I held tight and circled out of danger. I took a deep breath, hands still up in defense, found my balance, and regained my vision.

He came flying at me again. He threw a right. I stepped left and bounced. He turned, squared up, and threw another quick right. I dropped my level. His fist whiffed over my head as I shot forward, my right shoulder making contact with his thigh. I wrapped my arms around his legs and drove forward. He landed on his back. I rotated my hips, secured a side mount, and without thinking rained forearms onto his nose and face.

I was out of my element, throwing punches and forearms. I didn't know how many I should throw, how long I should continue, or if they would come and rescue the man lying beneath me. I stopped the blows and looked down at my opponent's bloody and battered face. Still in control and not knowing how this would end, I hopped to a full mount and threw a combination of punches. No one came to pull me off. No one came to stop the fight. I felt his chest heaving underneath my body, but he lay motionless. I didn't know if I should continue or let him go. I didn't know if they expected me to end the fight myself or if I would soon be pulled off by the referee. I regained my bearings, slowed my breathing, and stayed in control. Yelling from the crowd—profanity and innuendos— seemed to come alive. He stayed still under my body. I looked around. No reprieve was eminent, so I finally let him go and stood up. He was quickly enveloped by two men. They tried to revive him. He did not move.

John and Q jumped into the ring and wrapped their arms around me. "Mother fucker, you did it," John yelled. Q picked me up and twirled me in a circle.

The large man walked over, grabbed my wrist, and raised my hand in the air. "You put on quite a show tonight, man," he said flatly over the roar of the crowd. "I look forward to doing business with you."

I looked over and saw my opponent, conscious, sitting up, shaking his head, then turned back to the large man, relief overtaking me. "We'll see," I responded, pulling my hand from his grasp. I was fighting the urge to celebrate my victory. It didn't feel right, but at the same time, it was intoxicating. I could feel a tingling in my body, an energy flowing through me.

The large man turned and looked directly into my eyes, "You'll be back." He showed his patented tobacco-stained teeth through a sinister grin.

I looked back to the center of the ring. My opponent was now sitting in a chair in the far corner.

* * *

We walked out the door a half hour later with pats on the back from a room full of raucous, drunk strangers, and eight hundred dollars richer. As the welts on my face pounded, the adrenaline coursed through my body. I felt amazing. The endorphins filled me with everything I desired. I felt like I did after a tough practice, after I had battled head-to-head against the All-American teammate who kept me out of the starting lineup. Even though I didn't like pounding on a helpless opponent—

even though I didn't like seeing him lying unconscious in the middle of the ring—I felt full of energy. The adrenaline overrode any feelings of misgiving and I knew this was where I needed to be.

We got in the car and sat in the quiet stillness. I leaned my head back on the seat, reached my hand in my pocket, and pulled out the wad of cash I was handed just a few minutes before. I counted out four hundred dollars and reached my hand forward. "Here's your cut, guys."

"We didn't do anything," Q said softly.

"You were there for me—that's all I need—take it."

He nodded and took the money.

Chapter Eleven

I woke up on the floor in John and Q's silent apartment—my ribs sore—my left eye swollen, pounding rhythmically. I picked up my phone and texted my parents, letting them know I was staying with friends for the next few days. I walked over to the fridge, found a can of unopened soda, and placed the cold metal on my eye as I lay back down and drifted off. When I woke again, the two figures sat on the couch in their usual positions, set off in their own virtual worlds.

We spent the day hanging out, playing video games, and eating pizza. We talked little about the night before. Feeling a strange hangover and a slight tinge of disbelief, I ran what felt like a movie through my mind. I was up against the ropes, a blur of fists tagging my forearms, head, and torso. I saw myself tagging my opponent in the face with my forearm as he lay under me, blood dripping from his nose and mouth. I felt my hand raised in the air and the final words from the large man playing over and over in my head, "You'll be back." I heard his sinister laugh and saw his menacing smile.

I walked away after the fight, content, fulfilled, feeling good. But now, I had no desire to return, to put myself in that position again—being lied to, being played the fool. It turned out in my favor this time, but there was no guarantee I would walk away again. *What if they upped the game too far? What if they put me in a situation I wasn't prepared for?* I felt like a pair of dice in the large man's hands and I was not prepared to land on snake eyes, lying face down on a dirty canvas. As I sat there in the dim apartment with my newly anointed support team, belly full of cheese and pepperoni, the adrenaline had faded, the buzz of the fight, the roar of the crowd was miles away. The misgivings that were clouded by the rush of endorphins were now strengthened by the remnants of the fight on my face and body. Yet, later that night, while I played video games and my partners sat next to me smoking their share of last night's winnings, I could feel a pinging in my gut—a longing. I tried to suppress it, but no matter how hard I tried, the pinging became a gnawing—the gnawing became a pounding—the pounding a reverberating voice calling for more—reason finally giving way to desire.

I finally stood up. "Guys, I gotta go for a run."

"You can't sit still for a full day, can you?" John murmured through a haze of smoke.

"I just got to get up and move."

"Hey, man—go for it. You're the fighter."

I put on my shoes and took off into the night. I ended up running to my house. My parents were both asleep. I opened the door quietly and went into my room. I lay on my bed, trying to fight the urges within me. *I want to stay home*, I told myself. I knew I should fall asleep in my own bed and wake up the next morning to the smell of Mom's bacon and eggs. I shook my head. I argued with myself. I told myself to stay—to get back to my life. I knew what I should do. I knew the right path to take—but I got up and paced around my room.

I found my backpack on the floor and filled it with clothes. I grabbed my earbuds from the side table and my gloves from the chair beside my bed and put them in the front pocket. I tied my work boots together and hung them from one of the straps and then went to the bathroom and grabbed my shaving kit. I threw the straps over my shoulders, headed out the door, and ran the two miles back to John's place.

Along the way, I passed the field behind the apartments. I ran past the high school I graduated from just over a year ago and then the elementary school where I met Chan for the first time. I stopped running and pulled my phone from my pocket. I felt the need for my guardian angel again. I clicked on Chan's number and texted—*How's it going? Been awhile.* A warm wind blew through my hair. I walked for a block, looked at my phone— no reply. I sat down on the curb and let the warm night air relax my body. I felt a momentary reprieve from any urge, from my desires. I closed my eyes. I didn't know where to go. I didn't know who to turn to at that point. I had always kept a piece of myself a secret, away from everyone around me, even my parents, the ones who supported me through all my life's endeavors, the ones who drove me to all corners of the state as a young wrestler, and then later, paid my way to regional and then national tournaments. I wasn't even sure if I had ever been totally honest with myself.

But now, sitting there alone, I finally realized there had always been something hiding deep inside—some force that had a mind of its own. I noticed it a bit in college when I started filling my competitive desires with knock-out drag-out battles in the practice room every day. I needed the rush, but I wasn't aware just how badly I needed it.

My heart began to thump softly, slowly. I felt the tingling come back to my fingertips. I closed my eyes and tried to breathe the urge away. I breathed in. I breathed out. I breathed in and held it—and then let it out slowly. But the tingling remained and my heartbeat continued to thump. I stood up. I pulled my earbuds out and stuffed them in my ears. I searched for my favorite song, the song that pumped me full of adrenaline, the song that helped me through many miles on the road, training for the toughest competitions in the nation.

I put feet to pavement and banged out the remaining few blocks to John's place. I got to the front door and went in. They were engrossed in their own world as they were the first time, John rolling joints on the table across the room, Q, noise-canceling headphones blocking out reality, eyes fixed on the screen on the wall.

I walked over and sat on the couch, sweat rolling down my back, heart thumping, fingers tingling. I leaned my head back and closed my eyes. I relaxed for a moment and then pulled my earbuds out and opened my eyes. "John..." I called to the figure in his own world across the room. "Hey, John, " I called again. He turned his head halfway. "Find out when I can get another fight."

He nodded, smiled at me over his shoulder, and then focused his concentration back on more pressing matters.

Chapter Twelve

The next day I headed for work, knowing that there would be a few questions about the purple bruising under my eye, but I had been through this scenario many times growing up. I had my story well rehearsed and ready to go.

I walked to the office in the back of the store, grabbed a walkie-talkie, and went out to the yard. A few minutes later I got a call to load up ten bags of mulch and three medium-sized Arborvitae. On my way back to the yard, a lady stopped me and asked about potting soil. Not long after, I was with two other employees loading gravel into the back of a truck. The day seemed to be going by smoothly. I figured I might get through the day without having to answer any questions about my face.

After lunch, I was unloading bags of fertilizer when Big Jim came over to help. I found out early on that Big Jim wasn't named for his size, as he was not much bigger than me. "Watch out, man. I'm here to save the day," he sang loudly as if he were reciting a spoken word poem. "You look like you could use some help," he continued to bellow in cadenced song.

His nickname came from his jovial, outgoing persona. He wasn't afraid to get involved in any group activity or job or call attention to any of his so-called superpowers as he would load twenty-pound bags of mulch or sand or whatever, two or three high on his shoulders, and lug them endlessly around the storage shed, the yard, and the parking lot. "Hold on," he told me the first time I met him, "Let Clark Kent change into his blue tights and all this manure will be loaded before you know it." He laughed gleefully and joined in shoveling the brown pile over and over until the job was done.

Today, as we threw bags of fertilizer into a patron's trunk, he looked up at me and roared, "What you been up to?" He looked at me and grimaced. "Looks like your face ran into a Mac Truck."

"Looks worse than it is," I smiled, trying to make light of the black and blue that lay like clown makeup below my eye.

"Good to hear... 'cause it don't look too fun," he laughed as he threw the last two bags in and closed the trunk. "Hope you ain't putting yourself in harm's way." He winked.

"Nope. Just doing some off-season training in the mat room."

"Yeah—I heard you're the college wrestler."

I laughed. "Yep—got to keep in shape."

The day came to an end a little while later and a feeling of relief sat deep in my stomach as I hadn't run into my uncle who would have surely relayed the message of my messed-up face to my parents. I hopped on the bus and rode fifteen minutes to the gym and spent two hours soaking my workout clothes with sweat. I arrived back at the apartment around nine. My roommates were doing what they seemed to be doing every day, lighting up and spattering enemies' blood all across their virtual world.

I plopped down on the couch in between the two lifeless masses. "Anything to eat around here?" I asked, mingling my voice with the heavy silence. They sat, eyes glazed over, stuck in their own reality. I leaned over and pulled the headphone off John's left ear. "Anything to eat around here or do I have to get something?"

Without making an effort to acknowledge my reappearance in the room, he mumbled a couple incoherent retorts and flipped his headphone back on his ear.

I stood up and walked out the door. I leaned against the railing overlooking the vacant road outside the apartment. It was late, yet I was not tired. I was not ready to end my day. I walked down the stairs and out to the sidewalk. I began walking without knowing where I was going. I crossed the street and walked up two blocks toward the main road. A few cars drove by, heading to destinations unknown. The mini-mart down the road was mingling its yellow glow with the bright lights that lined the street with white circles at perfect intervals.

I set my sights on the yellow glow and soon found myself standing in front of a line of windowed fridge doors at the back of the store. I looked up and down each window until I came across the comfort drink I used to fill my dorm-sized fridge with last year in college, the VitaWater that quenched my thirst after a long practice or workout.

I purchased a six-pack of Glacier White VitaWater and three of my favorite protein bars and walked back to the apartment. The two blobs on the couch remained, so I found the corner I slept in the night before, lay down on a blanket and relaxed. I looked at my phone. It was just after eleven. I looked back at my phone a little while later and it was suddenly three o'clock. The room was quiet and dark. I sat up and looked around. It was deserted. I scrolled through my email and my news feed. I opened YouTube and typed—*backyard MMA*—and sifted through a myriad of videos. I watched a few crudely-produced matches. I didn't want to end up on the internet in one of these human cock fights, being yelled at by foul-mouthed drunkards. But, for some reason, it was still enticing. Partially, it was the rush of the crowd and the adrenaline pumping through my body, but I also left with a nice chunk of change in my pocket. I lay there trying to convince myself a couple more fights would be alright, trying to give myself a few reasons why it was okay— *I'm good, I can take care of myself. I was smart enough—aware enough of myself—I could do it for a couple months and then go back to school at the end of August.* I thought about the money. I thought about the roaring crowd. I thought about pounding and being pounded.

I went to work the next day. I went for a run when I got home. I went to the gym and lifted. I found a heavy bag in the back of the gym and practiced throwing punches. I made this my routine and decided I could train on my own. *I knew what I was doing*, I convinced myself.

Chapter Thirteen

Two weeks after my first fight, the three of us were back in the alley waiting for the large man and his driver to lead us to the next undisclosed location. This time we drove in the opposite direction and ended up at the back of a large wooden building at the end of a dark alley in an unknown area outside the city. There were already a bunch of cars crammed into a dirt lot as we pulled in and searched for a spot to park.

While my first fight was not held in Madison Square Garden by any means, it was a far cry above the place we had been led to this time. But even though I probably should have been questioning the locale—and the patrons of the night's events—my reticence had been put behind me. Once I had made the decision to continue fighting, I never gave it a second thought. I was going full steam ahead with no reservations—and mistakenly, with no questions asked.

An unmistakable stench of deviance filled the decaying ware-house. It reminded me of walking into a backroom poker game, a single light illuminating the table, a group of surly men hunched over their hands, smoke rising into the lampshade above. It was eerie, yet oddly intoxicating. I felt I was walking into the underbelly of a crime ring and I was the main attraction.

My body came to life. My fingers started to tingle. I felt

a smile emerge, slowly taking shape, filling my face. There was no private cell to warm-up in. There was no separation between me and the aberrance that stood surrounding the flat open space in the middle of the room where, currently, two mounds of beef pounded away at each other.

We stood at the back of the room. I used a small corner to prepare myself. John and Q stood between me and the masses who were currently jeering at the mess of lefts and rights entangled in the middle of the ring. I wondered why the large man brought me here. It seemed more than a few steps down from the previous fight. But, I focused and prepared as I would for a championship battle. I had learned over my years of competition not to underestimate any opponent, especially if I had never seen him before. So I approached this fight with the utmost focus.

The current fight ended and another began. I couldn't see the fight from where I was, but from the displeasure emitting from the crowd, I assumed it was much like the previous one.

The large man appeared. "Tonight is different," he explained. "The fighting may look poor, but the money is much better." He rubbed his hands together. "If you do your job, you'll find yourself in the final fight of the night. That's where the big money comes." He looked to the center of the room and then turned his attention back to me. "So, kick some ass so we can all go home happy." He walked off. John looked at me and shrugged. Q stood with a blank look on his face. I bounced up and down, waiting for my turn in the dirt ring in the middle of the room.

The next fight ended with obscenities and empty beer bottles thrown at the bloody gladiators as they vanished into the crowd. And then an unknown hooligan in dirty blue jeans and a hooded sweatshirt led me through the masses. Greasy hands pushed and patted me as I made my way to the middle of the room and onto the dirt ring. There was no announcer, just a single bellow calling for bets above the thundering crowd.

My opponent stood across from me. I was disappointed by the flabby belly and ripped blue jeans. I knew he had taken my place and was now the expendable one, there only to liven the crowd and fatten the pot. They wanted to see blood dripping from his face. They wanted to see him stumble, half dazed after receiving multiple blows to the face, and fall to the ground. They wanted to see me pounce on him and beat him senseless. And that's what I did. For the first time, I felt like a fighter. I stepped toe to toe with him, ready to throw punches and end the match—and his time in the ring—by any means necessary.

By the time he had thrown a few punches, he was breathing heavily. I danced around as he hopped in front of me. I landed two quick fists dead center on his nose. He wobbled backward into the crowd that hovered on the outside of the ring. Faceless hands pushed him forward, urging him to keep going. He seemed to gain a second wind, shuffling toward me and throwing awkward punches. I lowered my level, shot on his legs, and lifted him off the ground. I took him to the compact dirt with a thud and heard the air leave his body with a bellowed grunt. He gasped, trying to regain his breathing. I pounced into a full guard as he lay helplessly fighting for air, and rained fists down on his face, one after another.

A moment later I was grabbed, pulled off my victim, and my hand was thrust in the air. The wooden room was filled with bloodthirsty cries. I had woken the beast within and the beast was happy.

I looked down at my opponent. He was lying, listless and

bloody on the ground. Two men walked over and pulled him to the side. He sat in a crumpled, dazed confusion. I turned my attention back to the roaring applause. The tingling in my hands overtook my entire body. My chest grew two sizes as my ego took control. I bounced around the dirt circle waving my arms in the air, urging the crowd to continue their serenade.

John grabbed my arm. "Hey, let's go. You're gonna have another fight." He pulled me through the crowd as the next fight began. I turned to see two guys square off. I scoffed as they lumbered around the circle awkwardly throwing punches and stumbling into a clinch. One of the fighters locked his hands around the back of the other guy's head, hoisted a knee upwards, but ended up losing his balance and wobbled backward. "Don't pay attention to those guys." John yanked my arm. "Those fights don't matter. They're here to fill time. I heard Oscar talking to some dude about the main event. They got you fighting the winner from last week. They had it planned from the start." He looked at me with a seriousness I was not used to seeing on his face. "I know I don't know shit, but he sounds good. He clobbered a couple guys last weekend."

"What else did you hear?"

"Only that he sounds big. I don't know how big, but from what I can tell, bigger than you."

"How long 'till the fight?"

"Soon, man—after this fight they are going to take bets and then you're up." He looked a bit worried. "They only had you fight so they could set the odds for the main event and get people to put money on you."

"I've wrestled five and six matches in one day. I can handle another fight." I hopped up and down, adrenaline still pumping through my body. "The first one was not even a warm-up."

98

"Whatever man—just want you to know what's up."

"Thanks—that's what you guys are here for."

"You need anything?"

"Yeah—grab me a drink out of my bag. That should be enough."

We went back to my warm-up corner. I downed the drink and moved around to keep my body warm. The current fight ended and a thunder of commotion bounced off the ceiling. A man dressed in dirty Levis, work boots, and a black T-shirt stepped to the center. I could barely hear what he was yelling to the crowd, but I assumed they were taking bets for my next fight.

The large man's driver appeared in our corner. "You're up next." He waved his hand for me to follow. I raised my open palms toward my roommates. They slapped my hands, John yelled a nervous war cry, and I turned and bounded toward the dirt circle. I felt a slap on my back as I squeezed through the crowd, "Fuck him up, hombrecito," a raspy voice urged. "Pound his face," another voice rang out.

I stepped onto the dirt circle and saw a mound of muscle covered in tattoos, pacing back and forth like a caged lion, awaiting my arrival. He was at least four or five inches taller than me and at least a half-dozen years older. He was wearing a red pair of fighter shorts with a white stripe down the side and a look of disgust on his face, as if I were there to take his life and he was determined to take mine first. He looked at me and spat on the ground. I stood in one spot, bouncing slowly from one foot to the other.

There were no formalities before the fight began—no meeting in the middle of the ring to hear the rules and touch fists—just a faint voice, barely audible over the crowd, calling us to begin.

We stepped close to the center, moving back and forth, eyeing each other up and down. The closer we got, the bigger he looked. I knew he had me in size and weight. But as I watched him move I knew he had holes in his game. I knew he couldn't keep up with me. I could tell his feet were slow and he didn't have a clear game plan. I figured he was going to fight on instinct.

He threw a wild combination, but I was out of reach. I threw a punch to follow up, just missing the left side of his face. He moved closer with lumbering steps. I bounced quickly out of his way and tagged him on the right ear with a quick jab. He turned and looked at me as I hit him with a straight right. He pulled back, shook his head, and walked slowly from side to side, again watching me like a lion ready to pounce. I was sure he was used to a collision of action from the start and wasn't sure what to do. He stood tall and pounded his chest with both fists. I stood in front of him, out of reach, bouncing on my toes. I knew I had to figure him out before I attacked.

The crowd began to get restless. The noise began to erupt. He moved forward. I circled left. He followed my movement and tried to get close enough to strike, but without a cage or ropes behind us I was able to evade him with ease. The dance continued and he began to get frustrated. He darted toward me. I hopped to my left and caught him on the chin with a solid right. He charged forward again. I hopped to the right and hit him square in the cheek with a left. He charged a third time. I bounded to the right. He lost his balance and stumbled into the crowd. They caught him and shoved him back into the circle.

I knew I had to engage more soon. I could feel the angst of the crowd as the profanity began to fly. My opponent stood in the center of the ring and waved for me to engage. I took a few steps forward and bounced in front of him. I circled to my left and then to my right. I didn't want to make any rash moves, so I worked another angle.

I nodded my head and flashed a quick smile. I continued to bounce and reached my right fist out in front as if taunting him to come after me. I bounced one way and then the other. He stepped forward, I bounded back, keeping out of his reach. And there it was. I figured him out.

He stepped forward again, just like before. I stood my ground this time and waited. He took another step forward and raised his hands to strike. I lowered my level and shot for his legs, lifting him onto my shoulder and sweeping his legs out to the side. I brought him down to the ground and landed with my shoulder in his belly. He grunted, but quickly found his way to the guard and began pelting my ribs on both sides.

I was on both knees, between his legs. I placed my right forearm under his chin and applied pressure. His punches flailed and missed their intended target. I dug my left hand under his arm and blocked him from throwing any more punches. I used my right hand to throw repeated punches into the side of his face. He tried to use his free arm to block the blows, but I kept pecking away with my fist.

I changed to a hammer fist and brought it down on the brow of his nose, two—three—four times and kept going until I lost track. For some reason, I felt two hands grasp me from behind and bring me back to my feet. My opponent stood up, blood dripping from his nose and mouth. He took a deep breath and spit a mouthful of blood into the dirt.

The hands that pulled me up, pushed me to the center of the ring and the bloody man in front of me clocked me with a hook to the right side of my face. I was caught off guard. He hit me twice more and I staggered backwards. My mind went blank for a moment while I tried to figure out what was going on. He lunged forward out of control. I tried to move out of his way, but the dirt circle had shrunk. The crowd was now on top of us as we were forced toe to toe. He hit me again, and then a few more times. I tried to block his punches, but they kept landing on my face, in my gut, on the side of my ribs. I was taking more punishment than I had ever taken before. I pulled my hands close to my face. He hit me in my belly.

Finally, I was able to lunge forward and under his flailing hands. I grabbed a body lock, lifted him off his feet, and let out a guttural yell as I swooped him into the air and back to the dirt floor. This time I was not taking any chances. I sat on top of his hips and began punching him in the face with as much power and speed as I could manage. He brought his hands up to block my punches, but I kept them coming. I watched both of his hands fall back to the ground, lifeless. He didn't move, but I kept swinging away, pounding his face with everything I had.

Suddenly, I was tackled by the referee and it was over. My opponent lay there, lifeless for a moment, but then struggled to his hands and knees.

I was bombarded by the crowd and pulled to my feet. They surrounded me. They cheered and called my name. I looked around to find John and Q, but it was no use. I was stuck in the center of the melee. My heart pounded and the tingling overtook my body. I felt like I could fight again. I bounced on my feet and raised my arms. The crowd continued their explosive cheers.

I pushed my way through the crowd and back to my warm-up corner. I looked around and finally, John and Q came running at me. "Haha—fucken amazing," John yelled. Q lifted me up and gave me a squeeze.

"What the fuck was that?" I said, half enraged, half exuberant.

"I don't know, man, but I thought you were gone for a minute. But you picked that big mother fucker off his feet and thrashed him on the ground."

I sat on a chair in the corner and put my face in my hands. I took a deep breath, sat up, and let out a deep, prolonged cry. My roommates joined in my cheers. Our celebration got lost in the prevailing ruckus, but the primitive cry filled me with energy. I stood up and bounced around, letting the emotions around me fuel my body.

The large man and his driver appeared out of the crowd. "You ready for more?" the large man shot through his tobacco-stained teeth.

I stood up. "You got more?"

"Not tonight, my man. But don't worry. I've got plans for you." He reached out and handed me a fat, dirty envelope. "Take this and get your face taken care of. We'll be in touch." He nodded his head and the two men walked off and disappeared. John handed me a towel from my bag. I wiped the sweat from my body and the blood from my face.

By the time we got back to the apartment, the adrenaline was wearing off and my face and ribs were throbbing. I walked to the bathroom mirror and looked at myself. I smiled and shook my head. I closed my eyes and played the fight over in my mind. My heart rate quickened and, despite my pounding body, I felt good.

I took my clothes off and climbed into a hot shower. I leaned my hands on the wall and let the water run over my head, down my neck and body, and into the tub. I watched as the water washed the blood from my face and down the drain. I stayed there until the blood dissipated and the water was clear.

I got out of the shower, dried off, and pulled on a pair of shorts. I walked into the living room where everything was normal once again. The two lifeless masses were back on the couch, ears tamped shut, the smell of weed in the air.

I found some ice in the freezer and put it in a plastic grocery bag. I sat in between the two gamers on the couch and rested the ice on my face. I leaned back and felt my face slowly go numb. I rested there, letting my face sit under the ice, feeling the ice melt, droplets of water running down my cheek and neck, images of the night playing in my head.

I got up, put the ice back in the freezer, and went back to my usual corner. I searched through my bag for ibuprofen, poured a few tablets into my hand, and downed them with a bottle of Glacier White VitaWater. I sat for a moment and ate a protein bar and then turned over on my stomach and looked at my phone. I had a message. I clicked the button. Chan: *Sorry I didn't respond sooner. Everything is good here. Hope all is well with you.*

I turned onto my back and closed my eyes, allowing my body to relax. I took a deep breath and smiled.

Chapter Fourteen

Over the next few weeks, I continued my training and the Saturday night fights. The fights were held at different locations each time, yet the crowds, and the fighters, were much the same. I continued to go to work Monday through Friday, trying to stay incognito so my uncle wouldn't see the remnants of the fights on my face and tell my parents. I texted my parents once in a while in order to keep them at bay, letting them know I was working and training. I took advantage of their trust, and while I did feel guilty hiding my second life from them, the call of the ring overrode anything else in my life.

My time became a connection of laboring pursuits—daily work at my uncle's nursery, two hours in the gym in the evening, and fights on the weekend. I was fulfilled. I was doing everything my body craved. Hitting and being hit was all I wanted. I was becoming king of the warehouse fights and was getting my fill of adrenaline, but didn't realize that with each fight my tolerance was increasing. After a while, I was craving the punch, not just delivering, but receiving. Sometimes I would stand in front of my opponent and let him hit me two or three times, taunting him with a bloody smile before I attacked. Sometimes I would stand toe to toe and trade punches back and forth, gaining energy with each blow.

At the end of each fight, no matter what I looked like, I felt invincible. But the only thing that made me feel that way was the fight. I would go to work on Monday and what once was gratifying labor, was not enough. I found myself trying to find ways to increase the adrenaline as I worked. Carrying more. Lifting more. Running from one stack of mulch to another—lifting—carrying—running. Co-workers were amazed. They would ask me why I worked so hard or how I was able to lift so much. I would tell them that I was in training for college wrestling. Everything I did outside the ring was a cover story. Everything I did was a way to keep my second life a secret. I was a stereotypical addict. I had all the signs. I knew what I was doing was wrong, but I lied to myself and everyone around me, my parents, my Uncle, even John and Q who were the only ones who actually knew my second life.

My fourth weekend of fighting is when it started. The fight felt uneventful. Even though we had exchanged a few blows, I needed more. I needed a challenge. I didn't want to take him to the mat and end the fight. And so, I stood in front of my opponent and let him hit me three times. I moved out of the way and smiled. My head was ringing and I tasted blood in my mouth, but the noise of the crowd, and the adrenaline coursing through my body, drowned it all out. All I could feel was the tingling in my body, a euphoria that thrust me forward.

I threw punches. He threw punches. We stood there and exchanged punches back and forth. I stepped back and bounced around the ring, stopped, and smiled again. He came forward and threw a left and then a right. I moved my head and blocked them with my hands. I moved forward and pushed him up against the ropes. I struck his midsection with my left and then a right cross to his face. His head buckled. I bounced in place and watched him holding the ropes, shaking his head slightly. He staggered forward, trying to keep his balance. I could have ended the fight right there, but I wanted it to keep going. I gave him room to move. But he looked at me with glazed eyes. I came to understand that, unless he fell flat on his face, I would have to end the fight. There would be no standing eight count, no referee stoppage.

I stepped forward and took a quick shot, lifted him in the air and slammed him on the canvas. With three quick jabs to his face, it was over. He was done.

On the ride home that night John was concerned. "What are you doing, man? Just end the fight. Why did you let him hit you like that?"

"Just having some fun," I replied, matter-of-factly.

The following week, I fought a preliminary bout and didn't have a chance to prolong anything. His punches did nothing to me. I took a few and then threw three quick ones of my own, flit—flit—flit, and it was over. He fell forward to the ground. My first knockout.

My final fight of the night, what was supposed to be the money maker, a tall, burly linebacker stood across from me. My heart raced. An ominous grin rose on my face. I was ready to give and take, to feel and be felt. But two minutes in I was disappointed. He kept his distance. He knew if he got too close I could take him to the ground. He tried to use his length to land punches, but there was nothing behind them, he didn't have enough power and he was too far away. I stepped closer, my hands lowered to my chest. He backed off. I moved closer again. He didn't take the bait. He was using my tactics against me.

I charged, something out of character, but I needed a fight.

I knew I could beat him if I stayed patient, but all of a sudden, it was not about beating him. My body craved the drug and the only way to get my fix was through his fists. I drove him into the plywood that made up half the makeshift octagon that separated us from the vocal mob calling for the kill. I leaned against him and thrust my fists into his gut just enough to wake him up, hoping he would get angry and throw back. I brought a hand to his face with a thud and then stepped backward, waving him on. He looked at me with a scowl and walked forward, hands in front of his face. I stood there, feet apart, craving the impact. And there it was, his hands collided with my body, thwack—thwak—thwak. My body rejoiced.

I smiled within and returned his gesture—THUD—my fist met his face. He retaliated with two to my cheekbone and one to my ribs. We traded back and forth and a new instinct took hold. I started bobbing and weaving like a trained boxer. He threw. I dodged one way and clocked him with a jab. He threw again. I ducked, weaved, and hit him with a straight left and then a right hook. He staggered back. I pounced on him, throwing left-right combinations. He fell back on the ropes. I continued the barrage as he held onto the ropes with one hand, trying to stay on his feet. I stepped back. He stood there, half-conscious. I stepped forward and hit him with one last blow and watched him slowly sink to his knees—and then his hands—and then collapse to his side. I watched as he was pulled to the corner of the makeshift octagon. John and Q flew under the ropes and embraced me. They hooted and hollered. They spat obscenities. They danced.

I looked around hoping someone else would challenge me, someone else would jump into the lopsided octagon, tear off his shirt, lift his fists, and beckon me forward. But no one did and I was left unsatisfied.

I lay there that night, in my corner of the apartment, ice on my face and ribs, reading through the string of texts I had been sending back and forth with Chan for the last two weeks. Here was another cover-up. Here was another person I loved that I was keeping at bay, at arm's length, in my false reality. He was living a good life at UCLA, taking summer classes, studying aerospace engineering. Of course he was. He was always the smart one. He was always the one making the smart decisions, for both of us.

I still remember trying to coax him into coming to wrestling practice when we were kids and then trying to talk his parents into the idea. They always said he needed to focus on school. And they were right. But I didn't see it. I was the king of my private fight club. I was the one fighting for the loose change that filled my pocket after each scrap on the worn-out field behind the apartments. I didn't see what Chan was doing. He admired my fighting prowess, but he also knew he needed to be the conscience for both of us.

While I was training to be a wrestler, he was studying his math, his AP History, his college-level Chemistry, and Physics. I didn't know it at the time, but he was the one everybody should have been looking up to. I lay in my corner of the apartment, admiring him, missing him, wishing he was here or I was there. I wanted his guidance, but I could not be honest with him. I was ashamed of what I was doing, but I didn't know how to stop. So I stuffed that knowledge deep down and kept texting my fake reality. *Things are great here.* I lied. *Training for my second season.* I spun my yarn. *Shooting for a national title.* I continued my fantasy.

Chapter Fifteen

It was mid-summer and my gloved hands had just hoisted a bag of gravel onto my shoulder and loaded it into the bed of a small pickup. I had kept up my charade until this point, or so I had thought. I made my way behind the large storage barn at the back end of the nursery and began scooping gravel into a wheelbarrow with Big Jim when my uncle drove up in his F250. It was just two days after what was a rather easy weekend of fighting. He hopped out of his truck and called my name. Knowing I had a nice shiner under my right eye, one of many that had adorned my face the past month and a half, I ran my usual cover-up story through my head.

"Just wanted to say hi," he greeted me with a smile as I leaned my shovel against the wheelbarrow and shook his outstretched hand. "I don't get to see you much."

"I'm always shoveling something back here it seems."

"You do keep yourself busy. Everyone raves about how hard you work."

"Thanks," I looked down at the ground, "and thanks for the job."

"You deserve it," he said, patting my shoulder. "I'm glad you're here." He looked at me a bit deeper, "How's your training going?"

I looked up and wondered, for a moment, if he knew what I'd been doing.

"I assume that's where you're getting the black eyes."

"Yeah—uh—training's going well."

"I wanted to check up on you. I wanted to make sure you're okay because your parents said that you're not staying at the house anymore."

"Yeah—I'm staying with friends."

"Oh—whereabouts?"

"Close to the gym—easy access, you know."

"Of course—right." He looked at me for a moment. "You just training wrestling?"

"What do you mean?"

"I don't recall you getting this many black eyes from wrestling in high school."

"I've been trying some other stuff for fun—some boxing, some Jiu-Jitsu."

"Oh—for fun, huh? Not sure I would find that fun," he laughed.

"Well, maybe fun isn't the right word," I covered my tracks.

"I guess cross-training keeps it fresh."

"Right—it does—and boxing helps with footwork," I smiled. I was proud of my ability to think on my feet, to keep my secret life a secret.

"Okay—well, just wanted to check in with yuh. I've got to get to a meeting. Let's have lunch soon."

"Yeah—sounds good—I'd like that."

He hopped in his truck and leaned his head out the window. "I'll find you around the yard one of these days when things slow down." He winked and drove off.

I grabbed my shovel and rejoined Big Jim. "Leaving the

hard work for the pros?" he laughed and tossed an oversized shovelful of gravel into the wheelbarrow.

"Figured Superman could handle a pile of gravel on his own." I met his shovelful with one of my own.

We continued our banter until the pile of small rocks was transferred from one locale to the other while the sun beat down and hastened the sweat that soaked our shirts.

At the end of the day, I walked to the storage shed, put away my shovel and gloves, and then went to the office inside and put my walkie-talkie on the charger. When I re-emerged, I saw my mom and dad standing in the parking lot talking with my uncle. I grimaced and cocked my head. *No way I can get around this one,* I thought to myself.

I took a breath and walked what seemed like a mile across the parking lot toward the three figures who seemed to be hatching some sort of scheme. Thoughts raced through my mind as I got closer. *Maybe they knew more than I thought. Maybe I wasn't fooling anyone. Maybe they were planning an intervention.*

"Hey there stranger," my dad called out as I approached.

"Hey, Dad. What you guys doing here?"

"I'd like to say we were plant shopping, but we really came to see if you wanted to go out for a bite."

"Ah, well, I usually go to the gym after work."

"Come on. It's been a while. You can humor your parents for a short meal?" My mom smiled and put her arm around me.

"Sure—I can work out after," I replied, hoping to get them to drop me off at the gym so they didn't find out where I had been staying the past few weeks.

"Yeah—of course," she said, flashing me one of her mom smirks that sent me back about ten years.

"Well, Barry," my dad said to my uncle, "we'll come by and

pick up a couple of those grasses to fill that corner in our front yard," he winked.

"Okay—we should be getting a new shipment in by the end of the week."

Couldn't they be a bit less obvious? As if my uncle's earlier conversation with me and my parents showing up at the end of my shift were a coincidence.

I jumped in the back of the car and we headed to our family's favorite Mexican restaurant. A purposeful nostalgia builder, as we passed two perfectly good Mexican restaurants along the way.

"So," my mom turned around, "Berry said you're a great worker." She flashed me another motherly smile.

"Yeah—I actually enjoy the work."

"That's nice," she replied softly and the car grew quiet.

We stopped at a red light and the stillness added to a growing tension. It seemed to last forever before the car revved up and a soft rumble mingled methodically with the heavy silence. I wasn't sure if it was just me or if my parents felt the anxiety as well.

"What've you been doing besides work and going to the gym?" my dad's voice sliced through the pressure. "Anything interesting?"

I paused—"Not much. Just hanging with friends."

The silence quickly took over again. We sat there for the next few minutes until the car turned right and wound its way through the parking lot and came to a stop in front of Ricardo's.

We sat at our usual table, the table that my mom, dad, sister, and I sat at many times throughout our childhood.

"You want the super nachos to start?" my dad asked cheerfully as our glasses tinkled full of ice water with the waiter's tipped hand.

"Sounds good," I said, eyes buried in my menu.

We snacked on the obligatory chips and salsa as we waited for our food. Normally the conversation flowed easily at family meals, but I stayed distant, so I didn't give anything away. I felt, though, that my unusual behavior was alerting my parents to a secret hiding beneath the bruised exterior that lay openly on my face.

"So," I broke the silence with honesty, hoping to quell any suspicion, "this past year was tough." I kept my eyes down at the table. "I want next year to be better." Dad nodded his head slowly. Mom reached over and put her hand on mine. "It feels good to stay independent—to stay with friends," I added, not really knowing what else to say.

"We get that," my mom said.

"Yeah, son... We understand wanting your independence." He tilted his head, pursed his lips, and looked at me. "We support you on that. We just wanted to see how things are going."

Our food arrived and I let the warmth of the meal coat my belly and a feeling of comfort overtook me. Memories of birthday parties and family meals suddenly filled me with angst. I felt pulled between the solace of my parents' embrace and the adrenaline of the fight world. I sat across from the bosom of my sheltered middle-class life, yet the tingling started to fill my fingers and then my hands. I knew what I should do. I knew where I should go—what I should say. But my body started craving. My mind told me to get back in the car with my parents and go back to our house, to cozy up in my room. I knew what the right decision was, but my body told me something completely different. It told me to run out of the restaurant—to flee.

I held my ground and continued eating, hoping my parents were none the wiser, but I knew my second life was showing through. I tried to cover it up, "Thanks for the support. Training is going well. I feel I'm on track for next season."

"That's good to hear," my dad said. "We do have a couple questions, though." Heat rose through my neck and into my face. I was sure my pallor matched the salsa that sat on the table between us. "Your uncle has some concerns." He paused. "He's seen you come to work pretty beat up on a regular basis." He looked at me and raised his eyebrows in concern. "And it's not just the bruises on your face."

I took a deep breath. Excuses ran through my head. Cover-up stories quickly took shape. "I've changed up my training." I sat there. "I'm doing some boxing and some Jiu-Jitsu." I looked up. "I've been doing some sparring." I turned to my mom, tears filling her eyes. A lump formed in my throat. I knew they could see through me. I was sure they didn't know exactly what I was mixed up in, but they knew I wasn't being honest. They could see the change in my body. They could sense the change in my demeanor.

"Son—we love you," my dad continued. A look of sincerity rose on his face. "I also want you to remember what I've always told you," sincerity quickly dissolved into a resolute warning. "Make sure the risks are worth it. You don't want to miss out because of something that could have been easily prevented."

We finished our meal with few words and half an hour later I was getting out of my parent's car in front of the gym. The last thing I said to them was that I would keep in touch. But as I put foot to pavement, I knew I couldn't let them in on my secret life. In fact, I had to distance myself if I was going to continue down this path.

I tried to live the next three weeks as if all was normal. I would get up early on the weekdays, go to work, and then hit the gym each evening. I would follow the trail to the next weekend's fight and then spend all day Sunday recovering. No matter how badly I beat the other guy, I always came away looking worse for wear and I knew my situation was anything but normal. I started looking over my shoulder. I felt I was being watched. I tried to avoid my uncle at work. I stopped talking to my co-workers, fearing they would slip my secrets to him, and then they would eventually find their way to my parents. And, for those three weeks, I held it together. I followed my routine. I did what I needed to do in one life while craving and living within the other. Deep down, I knew I couldn't keep it up, though. I couldn't live two separate lives. I had to make a choice, but I wasn't in any condition to make the right one.

At the end of the third week, in a dark, dank, smoke-filled dungeon, beneath a moonlit sky, somewhere deep underground in the middle of nowhere, the decision was thrust upon me. I had lost track of how many challengers I had toppled—sometimes one a night—sometimes two—one night it was three. How many different battlegrounds had I stood atop, hands raised victoriously, walking around egging the unruly mobs to further applause?

I stood at the back of the room, having just downed another opponent. A subsequent fight had started. The crowd was growling, watching the action intently, as life passed them by, with glazed eyes, pupils dilated in the darkness or in reaction to the substances flowing through their bodies.

I stood alone, for the moment, and then felt a hand on my shoulder. The hand slowly moved down my back, caressing each muscle as it flowed like warm water to my beltline. I stood still and turned my head to the left. Eyes peered out from behind curly shoulder-length hair that obscured half a face from forehead to chin. The hand worked its way down until it lay softly on the skin of my right buttocks. The figure sidled in front of me, the hand followed, flowing along the corrugated ridges of my body and stopping on my hip. Eyes looked at me seductively from behind the curly hair. And then the large man's sinister laugh pierced the darkness. "Another good fight tonight, my friend." The figure backed off as the large man walked into my view. "It's time for a change." I learned pretty quickly to keep my mouth shut—so I stood there, waiting for the boom. "It's time we get you to a bigger stage. We need to get you to a place where you can make some real money—a place where someone will give you a real challenge. And money is drying up here. Everyone loves to watch you fight, but the odds don't pay off." He turned and muttered something incoherent to the figure who still stood near. "So," he turned back to me, "tomorrow, be ready to take a ride."

"Where we going?"

"Don't worry about that. Just be ready to fight." He was always cryptic. I'm sure it was from years of skirting the law, keeping everybody who shouldn't know, not knowing. It was the only way to steer clear, to stay safe. "Pack your bags and be at the warehouse at noon tomorrow. Just you. Don't bring your friends. You won't need them anymore." He vanished into the crowd. The figure followed.

I stood at the back of the room and listened to the rumble of the crowd while my conscience told me to leave and never return. And I knew I should trust the voice in my head. But when I got back to the apartment that night, I took a shower and started packing. I wasn't sure what I was going to need or how long I would be gone, so I stuffed everything I had accumulated in my corner of the apartment into my backpack and a duffle bag while John and Q did as they always did, one fusing himself with the couch and diving into his unreality, the other, sitting at the table in the corner, rolling his way to his altered state. Even though I was told to come alone, I tried to talk John and Q into going with me, but it was a struggle just getting them motivated enough to leave the apartment and give me a ride to the dirty cinder block building where it all began.

Chapter Sixteen

We drove up the drive with as much knowledge of what lay ahead as we had the first time the dirty cinder block building came into view. And there it was again, the building, an ominous reminder of the world I had been sucked into not two months ago. The car idled as I sat in the back seat frozen between my two lives while the two in the front were off in their own world. My mind was still, on occasion, trying to talk sense into me, and at this point, sitting in front of this monument of my new reality, the voice was futilely talking away—*turn around—have them take you home.* But, the tingling that had become all too common, that had become my compass pointing north, drowned out the voice in my head that had now become a meek noise in the background.

I scooted up in my seat and peeked my head between my silent partners. "Okay, guys." I looked from one to the other. "Thanks." John nodded. Q sat silently. "Not sure when I'll be back." I paused for a moment, not sure what I was expecting from them at that point, but just knowing they were in my corner, however innocuous they were most of the time, had been comforting.

Finally, Q turned. "Yeah man, good luck."

"I'll send you guys updates."

A short silence. "Cool. I'll miss watching you fight," John added, keeping his gaze through the front windshield.

I got out of the car, pulling my bags with me. I threw my backpack over one shoulder and walked to the front door. I stood for a moment, trying to decide if I should knock or walk right in, but couldn't make up my mind, so I knocked and then entered.

The waiting room was deserted, but I heard a noise coming from behind the door that led to the warehouse where I assumed they held fights, although I had never fought there. I walked to the door and pulled it open. A flood of light hit me in the face. I turned back, shaded my eyes with my hand, and shook my head. I walked in slowly, allowing my eyes to focus. What was once dark and hidden was now bustling with activity. Forklifts were moving boxes and a hive of workers were opening—sorting—and stacking. It was like walking into another world. I turned my head from side to side, trying to make sense of what I was seeing, trying to find a familiar face, and then felt a hand on my shoulder.

"Ahhh... you made it." The large man's voice fought to be heard over the noise. "I didn't know if you had the cojones."

He was accompanied by three even larger men. They stood behind him—silent, hands clasped behind their backs, legs a few inches apart, dark suits and reflective aviator glasses. The large man was dressed as usual, worn work clothes and work boots, his tobacco-stained smile at the ready. "Let me show you around the place," he said, putting his palm on my back and guiding me forward.

I followed the tour, a bit perplexed, wondering why he was showing me this. I thought I was only the gladiator to be brought out in front of the crowd and to line his pockets with money. But I did as I was told.

We finally ended up in a windowless office that contained a beat-up wooden desk and a couple old chairs. His bodyguards stood outside the door. He sat behind the desk and gestured for me to take a seat. I set my bags down and sat just as the phone rang. The large man answered gruffly and began bellowing into the receiver. I sat quietly listening to the dull sound of machinery through the walls and the large man's voice rise and fall with emotion. From the few words I could understand I pieced together a story in my head—plane ticket—fighter injured—delay.

He hung up and set his phone on the desk. "Well, my man." He perked up unexpectedly. "We got some big plans for you."

Who's we, I thought to myself.

"We're going to fly down south. They got better fights and better money. A chance to make it big."

I sat there for a moment, not knowing what to think. "You mean legitimate fights?" I finally asked.

"Good fights, man," he growled, "good fighters." He showed his tobacco-stained teeth. "Just what you need to make it, man." He looked at me. "Yeah, legitimate fights… don't worry. I got you covered."

For some reason, even though I knew his idea of legitimate fights was not the same as mine—was not the same as the prize fights my dad used to watch on ESPN when I was growing up—I was drawn in, both by the mystery of it, as well as the anticipated rush of adrenaline my body craved. I didn't care where my next hit came from—in a back alley, in the basement of an abandoned building, or the Taj Mahal—I just wanted that hit.

"You see what's going on behind you?" He pointed to

the chaos in the warehouse behind the closed door. "Legit business." He paused. "Don't worry. We're all legit here." He winked and then stood up. "We're gonna take off in a couple hours." He walked to the door, opened it, and yelled some instructions to his bodyguards. He came back in and put his hand on my shoulder. "I got something to help you relax in the meantime."

A moment later, the figure with curly shoulder-length hair that approached me after my last fight, walked seductively into the room and sat on the corner of the desk. The large man leaned back in his chair. "Be ready, my man." He smiled his gritty smile. "This next step you're taking is going to be monstrous." He nodded his head at the figure on the edge of the desk. The figure took my hand and led me out of the office and into a dark room on the other side of the warehouse.

We spent an hour together before I fell asleep on a dusty old couch in that dark room. I felt awkward at first, but the figure's role in this new leg of my journey was evident, and that was something I wasn't going to fight. It had been a while since I had been intimate with anyone. It was just before winter break eight months before. I was at a party in the basement of my dorm—music was thumping—the lights were low. I looked across the haze of people gyrating in the middle of the room and noticed a familiar face—a girl who had drawn my attention in my freshman English class. She was leaning up against the wall, eyes closed, moving her hips to the thump-thump of the music wafting from the speaker sitting just a few feet away from her. And for some reason, after a tantalizing hour, doing things I had never done before—being pleasured by an alluring figure that had still to that moment remained nameless—I had fallen asleep on that dusty old couch in that dark room on the other side of the warehouse and dreamt about the girl from my freshman English class.

I was startled awake a little while later. The large man's driver was standing at the door as I lay there on the dusty old couch. "Rise and shine. It's time to head out," he barked. I grabbed my bags and followed him through a bustling horde of workers and machinery. We walked out an open garage door to the field behind the warehouse where the weathered ring and vacant seats remained exactly how they were the first day I was introduced to my new life. We loaded into an old gray SUV, just the four of us—the large man—the large man's driver—the nameless figure who had just spent the better part of an hour devouring me from head to toe—and me. But, when we came to a stop at the departures drop off at the airport, the large man turned and handed me a ticket with the instructions "to wait outside baggage claim when I arrived. You will be picked up by a man who will know who you are."

Ninety minutes later, I was alone on a plane, looking out the window at the endless farmland below. I knew the general direction I was headed, but where I ended up was out of my hands. My gut was filled with conflicting emotions—nervous uncertainty and unbridled anticipation gurgled within. I knew I should be weary, I knew I should take control over what was happening, but that was what made this so tantalizing. I couldn't wait to be pushed off the edge into the next adrenaline-filled abyss. Feeling out of control was in one way nerve-wracking, but in another—and the more thrilling part—it was heart-poundingly intoxicating.

I closed my eyes and allowed myself to drift away—to fall deep into reverie, into images of the past, to dreams of what's to come.

I woke up as the plane touched down. I was dead to the world for the past few hours, dreaming of my life and allowing my mind to march with the stars, building a new life among the dark trenches that provided me the drug that satisfied my urges. I opened my eyes to an unknown future—a future that I couldn't predict, yet craved. As I slowly allowed my presence to mingle with reality, I didn't know whose reality I was living. I was once the boy who traveled with family and teammates across state and country, in a highly regimented trek toward goals and achievements that were the only thing that seemed to matter. But, there was always another reality that lurked in the shadows, the one that thrived on the life lived on the field behind the apartments, that fought for loose change thrown at the end of each bout, that craved battle wounds, that loved to hit and be hit, to bleed, and draw blood. I had always kept him hidden, but now he had taken the lead and my former reality was buried deep in the recesses of my subconscious. And I was soon to find out that this was the way it had always been. My true identity was the fighter, the other, a weaker alter ego that stood no chance.

I found myself waiting outside baggage claim remembering the large man's instructions that I would be "picked up by a man who will know who you are." So, I grabbed a drink out of a vending machine and waited. And miraculously, as I sat, a man walked up and introduced himself. The man, tall and skinny with a few days' growth on his face, escorted me to a car not far away and, again, I found myself looking out the window in anticipation. It was hot outside. The sun was beating down on the dry earth and as we drove further, the paved streets and tall buildings gave way to rough roads and expansive fields.

Eventually, we turned onto a long gravel drive that took us

past worn outbuildings and barns. A few men were huddled around a small stable watching a lone man riding a horse. We drove past what appeared to be a field of wheat followed by a few acres of corn before coming to a stop inside an open garage. The tall man got out, walked around the car, and opened my door. He took my bags and led me to the main house, bound by wooden pillars and a wrap-around porch, the brick facade faded from years of sun exposure.

He set my bags by the front door and started back toward his car, but stopped, "You'll find your room on the top floor next to the bathroom. Someone will be by shortly to show you around." And then he was off, leaving me in the middle of nowhere.

I grabbed the handle on the screen door and pulled nervously, a rusty squeal echoed into the air. I knocked and waited. I knocked again. And then, turned the knob on the door, pushed slowly, and peered in. "Hello?" I questioned the deserted foyer.

I picked up my bags and walked in. A sparse, well-kept home, built in the early 20th century. The smell of dust and the worn furnishings swept me back to my grandparent's house many years ago. I expected to hear my grandma's voice calling me and my sister in for a meal, the standard meat fair and potatoes, with some sort of pie for dessert. It was odd. It diverged from my expectations of tough men, ill-kept, and foul-mouthed ready for the next human cock fight, waving dollars in hand above their heads.

I suppressed my urge to sneak about and peer into closed doors. Instead, I carried my bags up a set of creaky stairs flanked by a decades-old banister that seemed to speak to me as I slid my hand along its contours up to the second floor. At the top of the stairs was a bathroom and a storage closet to the right. To the left and next to the bathroom was a bedroom. I walked in, assuming it was mine for the time being. I tossed my bags on a table next to the bed and walked over to the lone window that looked over an expanse of live oak trees and corn fields. There was no life in sight, save for an eagle playing with soft white clouds.

I felt I could lie down and sleep through to the next day, but had a gnawing feeling I needed to stand ready. I wasn't sure what was going to happen next. For all I knew, someone might show up at any moment, whisk me away, and toss me into my next fight without warning. I rummaged through my bag and pulled out a pair of shorts, a T-shirt, and my running shoes. Whenever I didn't know what my next move needed to be, I always hit the road and put miles in between me and my current state of mind.

I slipped into my workout gear, stuffed my headphones into my ears, and went downstairs and out the front door. I took a cursory glance at my surroundings and headed down the remainder of the gravel drive that passed the house and disappeared into the horizon. I let a soft beat flow through my head and take me away as I listened to the rhythmic crunch of my feet reverberate through my legs and up my body. No matter where I was or how I was feeling, I was one with myself whenever I allowed my feet to move me forward at a good pace.

I ran within myself, without haste. I took the time to gather my thoughts, to ready myself for battle. While I didn't know what was around the corner, I did know at some point I would be thrust into the ring. I prepared as if I was readying for a world title, focusing my mind, relaxing my body as I ran.

I continued without knowing where I was going, without knowing how long or how far. I ran smoothly. I ran brisk. And then, I ran hard. I turned around and headed back to the house picking up speed as the sun faded. I used the final rays of dimming light to guide me back as my feet skipped across the gravel path. My arms churned. My chest heaved. I felt my feet floating inches above the ground as I sped up, bounded, danced, flew back to the ranch home in the middle of nowhere. The garage by the house came into view—I pushed myself harder. I felt my chest heave in and out. My legs moved—chest heaved— arms churned. I passed the garage, slowed to a jog, then a walk. As my breathing slowed, I let curiosity guide me on a walk around the house. I figured if nobody was going to show me around I might as well do it myself.

Behind the house sat a large storage shed. I walked up, cupped my hands on the small window at the top of the door and peered in, then opened the door and stepped inside, feeling around to find a light switch. I felt a string hanging in the middle of the room and pulled. A dim light illuminated a heavy bag, a few rusty free weights, and a small gray mat in the corner. I patted the heavy bag with my fists, left—right—left. Dust puffed into the air and floated beneath the light. I picked up two ancient dumbbells and pressed them over my head a few times and then set them back down.

I sat on a wooden chair in the corner of the room wondering what I was doing and what I had gotten myself into. The voice in my head was quietly trying to figure out what was going on as well. I could hear it churning questions around over and over. I closed my eyes and shook my head, trying to calm the little voice, so I could focus on surviving my current circumstances. I took a deep breath and looked at my phone. Three unanswered texts from my mom and dad. I saw their faces in front of me. I questioned my decisions. I questioned the desires that got me here. But then I stuffed the phone, along with my questions, and the little voice, back into my pocket, music still playing in my head. I leaned back in the chair and let the rhythms relax me. I closed my eyes. I took repeated breaths. And finally, the music ended. I removed my earbuds and left the ancient shack, the musty smell trapped in my nostrils.

When I got back to the front of the house, three men were standing by a truck near the garage.

"Yo, there's the man of the hour," one of them said in a distinctive southern drawl. "We've been looking for you." He smiled and took a couple steps toward me. "You checkin' the place out—whatcha think?"

"I just went for a run down the drive."

"Of course you did. You're our new champion. Gotta keep yourself in shape." He laughed and looked at his two friends. "You find your room upstairs?"

"Yeah—I put my bags up there."

"Good. Make yourself at home"

"Is that shack the only place to work out?" I pointed around the back of the house.

"Work out? Nobody's worked out in that shit hole for years."

"Oh—so—what do I do?"

"You wanna work out, you go down to the barn that's up that way," indicating the direction with a nod of his head. "The big one you passed on your way in. It's about a mile down the road here."

"When can I go?"

"Man, anytime you want. This place is your playground. Your only job here is to stay in shape and fight."

I smiled and nodded.

"By the way, my name is Jorge. This here is Jefferson—and this is Manuel." He pointed with his thumb to his left and then his right.

"Nice to meet you," I said hesitantly. They both laughed.

"No need to be formal around here," he smiled and patted me on my back. "I'm assuming you haven't ate much. Let's get you inside and fill that belly. Gotta keep the fighter fed."

Chapter Seventeen

I woke up the next morning with a ray of light shining through the window and alighting on my face—and a full stomach from the late-night meal I had with my hosts. I got up, dressed, and looked for my phone, which I was sure I had put on the side table next to my bed. I searched my bags. I looked under the bed. I checked the bathroom. But it was nowhere to be found, so I grabbed my headphones and headed downstairs.

The house was vacant. I went outside to the porch and looked around. Nobody was within eyesight, so I jogged up the gravel drive toward the barn where I was told I could work out. Off in the distance, I could hear equipment being put to use, and soon I saw my three hosts standing next to a corn field watching a large combine move down the rows of green stalks.

"There's the fighter," Jorge yelled my way. "How you feeling this morning?" He shot me a smile I wasn't sure I trusted.

I nodded. "Can't believe how hot it is this early."

"Yeah—you ain't a Southern boy, are yuh?" He laughed. "You'll get used to it after a while."

I tried to stay composed as questions rattled around in my head. *After a while?* My head started spinning. *What the fuck does that mean? How long are they planning on keeping me here?* I shook my head and looked at Jorge, "Have you seen my phone?"

I waited for a moment. "Did I leave it downstairs after dinner?"

He looked at me and shrugged, "Phone?" He turned his attention to a ruckus in the maze of corn and then turned back to me. "Don't worry about your phone. No need for a phone out here." He turned his attention back to the corn.

I took a deep breath and tried not to show my suspicions—suspicions I knew should have been peaked long before—before I found myself sitting in the large man's office twenty-four hours ago and then subsequently dropped off, alone, at the airport. So many indicators were steering me square in the face—slapping me silly more like it—clear as day. But my desires got the best of me—my need for adrenaline, for the drug that fulfilled my cravings, clouded my judgment, and the other self, from the other reality who used to be in control, was somewhere lost in the fog. The fighter was in charge now. This was a different self, the other self, from my new reality.

"We're going to get you set up here—get you comfortable," Jorge nodded. "Tell us what you want and we'll get it for you." Still trying to hide my angst, I mentioned some of the foods I wanted for my training, my favorite Glacier White VitaWater, some protein bars, bananas, chicken breasts, and veggies. "You got it, my man. We'll be sending a guy into town this afternoon."

An incoherent voice bellowed from the middle of the corn maze. Jorge held a flat palm in the air and the three men disappeared into the green abyss.

I walked to the wall of stalks and looked in. My hosts were gone. I turned around and put my hands on my hips, scrunched my eyes and looked at the few soft clouds floating in the sky. I took a deep breath and let it out slowly and then turned and headed to the barn. It was still a ways off, so I jogged, tucking the worries deep in the recesses of my mind, hoping I would find what I needed when I reached my destination—hoping I would start to get a better idea of my current situation. But when I opened the weathered door all I could see was darkness and a dirt floor covered in hay. My worries quickly resurfaced.

There was a rickety wall about ten feet inside. On the far left of the wall was another door. I pulled—the old hinges sprang to life, but fell flat inside a small room. I stepped in and followed a sliver of light. It led into a larger room that was illuminated by windows above cobweb-filled rafters. I turned a three sixty, amazed by what I saw. A line of weight machines was on the left wall. Dumbbells were organized along the far end. And two treadmills sat on the wall to my right next to a climbing rope hanging from the ceiling. A second rope, connected to the base of the wall, lay on the floor. In the middle of the room, a cage, an octagon, at least thirty feet in diameter, surrounded by beat-up, blue accordion gymnastic mats, fading from previous use.

"What a setup—an MMA gym," I declared to the empty room. I walked around, touching everything in front of me as if I was trying to convince myself it was not a dream. I found a heavy bag on the wall near the treadmills and a speed bag by the dumbbells. An old boombox and speakers sat in a corner off to itself. I pointed my finger and hit the red power button. A stack of CD's filled a small shelf. I found a few to my liking and set them off to the side and inserted a familiar disk into the tray. The soft gong serenading the death of Bon Scott filled the room—bongggggg—bongggggg—bongggggg—bongggggg—followed by Angus Young's iconic electric guitar solo. I bobbed my head and sang along with Brian Johnson, "I'm a ruling thunder, pouring rain. I'm coming on like a hurricane. My lightning's flashing across the sky. You're only young, but you're gonna die..." I was flooded with memories—car rides to tournaments with my dad, blasting and singing out of tune— "Hell's bells—Yeah, Hell's bells..." I climbed into the cage and began my ritual pre-fight dance, hopping from foot to foot— bounce—bounce—hop—bounce—bounce—hop. I threw jabs into the air, all nervous energy and suspicions vanished as I was taken back to a life that was far away.

The song ended and the next track began. I exited the cage and walked over to the dumbbells lined on the wall. I spent the next thirty minutes tirelessly pulling and pressing, feeling the blood course through my veins and my muscles fatigue. I hopped on a treadmill and ran. I ran for what seemed like miles, but did not keep track of time, distance, or speed. I just felt the beating of my heart quicken and the puff of my breath going in and out of my puckered lips.

Sweat poured from my forehead, dripped from my chin, flew off the ends of my hands as they churned back and forth faster and faster. Soon my shirt was drenched and my chest heaved in and out.

I slowed the treadmill to a jog and then a walk, and then got off and walked around the dirt floor of the barn. The music stopped and the only sound was the muffled hum of the combine off in the distance.

I sat on a rusty chair in the corner and listened to the methodical hum and a quiet voice in my head that started to wake up. My other self, from the other reality, peeked into this reality and asked questions. He tried to make sense of my current circumstances. He wondered why my phone went missing and why there was so much mystery surrounding me.

He tried to break through from one reality to the other and knock some sense into the self I had become in my current state. But I stood up and left him behind. I stood up and walked out the front of the barn back into the sun, back into the life I was choosing—the familiar tingle returned to my fingers. I stood outside the barn for a moment before heading back to my room in the old house that reminded me of my grandparents.

I walked into the kitchen. There were three cases of my favorite Glacier White VitaWater and boxes of assorted protein bars and bananas sitting on the counter. I opened the fridge and found everything else I had asked for. I opened a case of VitaWater, grabbed two protein bars, and headed up to my room. I plopped on my bed and filled my body with needed sustenance. A feeling of comfort floated through my body and the meal became an intimate experience as it grounded me in a visceral feeling of familiarity.

The next three days were a revisit of the day before. I woke up, found my three hosts somewhere doing something or other next to one of the fields, and then spent the morning in the barn listening to 80s rock and working out all my misgivings, stuffing them deep down where my other self in that former reality lay dormant. The rest of the day I read one of the three books I had in my bag or wrote in my journal trying to keep myself focused on goals I wasn't sure still existed. Before dinner on my fourth day, I walked the endless fields exploring all their cracks and crevices, one time finding a barbed wire fence that seemed to separate this estate from their next-door neighbors as I could see a set of barns and what looked to be a sprawling farmhouse on the adjacent side off in the distance.

Each night I found myself visiting my other self in the dark creases of my mind. Memories floated to the surface when my current self was less aware, less able to push them aside and stuff them away. But each day, I worked harder than the next, sweating away in the barn to keep myself in shape, and to keep my two selves apart. I would emerge from the barn, adrenaline flowing, fingers tingling and my former self would be sufficiently locked away.

It was on the fifth day that the reason for my presence on the farm was revealed to me. I didn't get any better picture of what went on at the farm or where it was actually located, but I knew what my role was to be. As I walked downstairs ready to start what had come to feel like my own personal Groundhog's Day, I found two men sitting in the living room, but didn't recognize either of them. They were cleanly dressed in dark slacks, a T-shirt, and sports jacket, one a dark gray and the other a navy blue. The man in the gray jacket looked up briefly and motioned for me to sit as if we were already acquainted and he was expecting my arrival.

The mysterious duo was different from anyone I had met so far—since finding my way into the fight game. They had an air of arrogance that escaped everyone else. The large man who set me flying to points unknown was gruff and unrefined, his driver, much the same. My three hosts were carefree, distant, and displayed the rawness that came with living miles from civilization. The man in the gray jacket and his partner in crime, to be known as the man in the blue jacket since I knew nothing else, were sophisticated, their speech filtered of the stereotypical, southern twang, filled with euphemism, yet also the decadence of the fight world.

They continued their conversation as if I wasn't there. "Yes, that's how I see it as well," the man in the gray jacket replied to a statement by the man in the blue jacket. "I also think they can wait for a week before investing that much money. They need to make sure the investment is feasible."

"True," the man in the blue jacket agreed. "But if they wait too long, the opportunity may pass them by."

"Were being remiss," the man in the gray jacket turned to me. "We need to welcome our guest." He stood up and extended his hand. I stood and met his hand with mine. He named himself and his partner and then, formality was over. "So, how are you liking your accommodations?"

"Uhh—yeah—nice—I guess."

"Sounds like you've been training hard. Jorge's been keeping me up to date."

"Hmmm—okay—yeah, I've been making use of the barn." My other self was fighting his way to the front, trying to push my current self out of the way so he could take control of the conversation.

"Are we missing anything you need?"

"No. I'm fine for now."

"So, you're probably wondering what you're doing here?"

"Yeah, I can do without the mystery," my former self butted into the conversation. Yet, my current self shoved him down and stood firmly in the foreground. "But I'm looking forward to fighting."

"Good," he looked at me curiously. "So then let's do away with the mystery." He looked at the man in the blue jacket and pointed his index finger at him.

"We saw your last two fights," the man in the blue jacket stated, "and we were impressed." He smiled, not the dirty smile of the large man, but a clean, reassuring smile, a trusting smile. "And we both agreed you deserve bigger fights and a chance at a bigger payday." I nodded and listened. "That's why we brought you here. You're our fighter. We believe in you, so we invested in you."

My other self perked up again and fought to the front, "Invested?" my other self asked. "What does that mean exactly?"

"Well," the man in the blue jacket responded, "We purchased your rights and paid the money to fly you here. And we paid to enter you into the premier fighter tournament."

"Hold on a minute," my former self could not be held back. "I wasn't informed of any of this. I was under the impression Oscar would be involved. Where is he?"

"Oscar?" the man in the gray jacket interjected. "Oscar is small time. He got his payday. Now you're with us and you're ready to have your payday."

My other self took a step up in my mind. *I'm being bought and sold like a head of cattle,* he told my current self. He took a breath and directed himself at the two men, "So, explain to me what I'm getting out of this. Up until this point I've only seen a change of scenery."

"Oh, man—this is why we got him," the man in the gray jacket turned to the man in the blue jacket and laughed. "He's feisty." I saw a fire erupt in his eyes, a fire that overtook his aforementioned sophistication, and his underbelly was revealed—his true identity—his lustful nature.

"Let's make this easy to understand," the man in the blue jacket said as he walked over to a table on the other side of the room and picked up a briefcase. He walked back, sat down, and set the briefcase on the coffee table between us. He opened it and turned it toward me. It was filled with piles of hundred-dollar bills. "This is yours. This is what we call your signing bonus." A darkness filled his eyes and the gravity of the situation changed immediately. "This is only the beginning.

You do yourself proud and you walk away a rich man. You will never have to work another day in your life." The room was silent as they let everything sink in.

"This may sound like a stupid question," my other self said, "but what do I have to do in order to walk away a rich man?"

"You do what you always do—win," the man in the gray jacket said nonchalantly.

My other self weighed his next question carefully, just as my current self piped in, "That sounds nice." My former self pushed my other self to the side. "But I need to know what I'm signing up for," my former self added, trying to stay in control. "Tell me about the fights. What do I need to prepare for?"

"Good for you. You have fire." The man in the gray jacket moved up in his seat and leaned forward. "Let's lay the cards on the table." I met his gaze, furrowed my brow, and leaned forward. "Your first fight is tomorrow night. You win, you'll have another fight in about five days. You make it to the finals you'll have a total of five fights. First fight is ten thousand. Double it each fight. And this is just the beginning. You win the whole thing, you'll have a chance to win more."

"Win more?"

"Millions?"

They leaned back in their chairs and looked at me as if they expected me to thank them, but I sat silently, my head spinning, my two selves feeling like they were drunk.

"That's it for now," the man in the gray jacket said. "Jorge will deliver you to the fight tomorrow evening."

They stood up and began to leave. The man in the blue jacket put his hand on my shoulder as he passed. "We have faith in you," he said. And then they left.

* * *

I worked out twice as hard that morning and went to bed excited that night, fingers tingling, dreams full of anticipation. I knew I was getting into something I might not be ready for—something I'd never seen before—but that is where my current self thrived, in the world of the unknown, in a world of anticipation.

Chapter Eighteen

After the sun faded the next day, my three hosts, dressed as if they were going to the opera, drove me to a different stratosphere about sixty minutes from the farm. We pulled into a circular drive in front of a large sprawling estate. We got out of the car and Jorge handed his keys to a gentleman dressed in all black who drove off without a word. I followed my hosts into a large marble entryway and then through a maze of hallways and down a set of stairs that led to a basement auditorium. I stood for a moment and looked around, my head spinning. I was in disbelief. It felt like we just walked onto a movie set. A fight cage sat at center, bound by formally set tables and chairs, an enormous chandelier hung overhead. I thought maybe we had ended up somewhere on Madison Avenue in New York City, but I knew we were still somewhere in the southern reaches of the country.

I had a hunch I was to be the entertainment for the one-percenters who filed in and found their seats at the silken-covered tables spaced regularly around the outside of the cage—but was I the court jester or the gladiator in the center of the coliseum—the one to be laughed at or the one to be admired and rained upon with roses? One thing I knew, though, I was no longer fighting for the working man as I walked past women in fur coats and men in dark suits. A small casino was set up on the far side of the room. Workers, wearing white dress shirts, black vests and ties, were shuffling cards and sweeping the felt on roulette tables. They were preparing for the onslaught of what I assumed would be millions.

I was led past an expansive bar that filled the entirety of the back wall of the auditorium, illuminated by a light shining above a mirrored shelf filled with sparkling bottles, and into a private locker room in the back corner. "Get ready here," Jorge instructed. "We'll stand watch." I took a few minutes to clear my head before I began my pre-match ritual. I worked to get my mind on track, away from the spectacle and onto the upcoming fight. Forty-five minutes later, I was back in my familiar state, sweat covering my body, ready to go. I paced around the room, gathering my thoughts, and then sat down. A grizzled, gray haired man, joined me in the locker room. He introduced himself as my cornerman. He reached out with his arthritic fingers, years of life visible on each protruding knuckle, half his left thumb missing, and proceeded to tape my hands and explain the rules of this new multi-million dollar game—*It didn't matter where the fights took place*, I thought to myself, *they were all the same*—When he was done, he patted my hands for good measure and left.

He popped his head in a few minutes later. "You'll be up soon," he said and then looked back out. He turned back and barked a warning, "Be ready. The crowd's getting restless. They'll be calling for someone's head soon." He looked out again—"Okay, you're up." He gestured for me to follow and led me into the moneyed arrogance of the waiting crowd. My three hosts, still on watch, followed behind as I headed toward the cage. It was eerie and dark—only the cage at center was visible under the chandelier. Quiet conversation floated over cocktails and caviar. The clinking of glasses and silverware accompanied me through the tables of diners who paid no attention. The curious absence of obnoxious drunkards, flying beer bottles, and profanity was odd. I almost missed the wild energy of the unruly mosh pits I was used to fighting in front of.

I approached the cage, my hands tingling, my heart pounding. I hopped up three steps and through the open gate. I jogged around twice, then stopped in the middle and bounced softly from foot to foot as my opponent made his way in. *I guess we don't have weight classes*, I thought to myself as a large burly figure strutted in. *Big and soft*, I smirked—but I knew better than to take anyone at face value—especially at this venue. *Who knew what type of talent their money could buy?*

A booming voice bounced off the porcelain walls and reverberated around the room. I lost track of everything as my eyes focused on the tub of muscle lumbering from foot to foot on the other side of the canvas. I sized him up and began devising a strategy. I wasn't sure what to expect from him, but I knew what I was capable of and focused on that. We were brought to center with more formality than my previous fights in the dark warehouses in the outskirts of my hometown. Muffled words were communicated by a man in a striped jersey as I started having a difficult time focusing on anything except my own voice echoing in my head. My previous self, from my former life was lost somewhere in the background as my current self was at the forefront of my mind, hopping up and down, ready to go.

We bumped fists and backed off. A bell rang off to the side and the fight commenced. As always, in unfamiliar situations, I took it slow—bouncing and circling, keeping my distance. He had reach. He had size. And, from the looks of it, he had power. If he caught me clean, with his right or his left, who knows how my body would react. I wasn't going to allow him to hit me in the face, if I could avoid it, however much I was craving the adrenaline rush.

I continued bouncing methodically, circling one way and then the other. And through my own voice in my head, I could hear my corner man's warning coming to life... "The crowd's getting restless." It was easy to sense that this was a common theme among the underground fight fans, no matter their economic means.

The lumbering man across from me began to plod forward, this way and that, trying to cut off my angles and catch me against the chain link walls. As he got closer, I darted under his outstretched arms as he threw a few obligatory punches into the air. I circled away and hopped in place. I felt the tension rise and the cage seemed to shrink, as if we were being pushed together by some invisible force. But I stayed to my plan. I waited to figure him out. I waited to see how he moved. After a couple minutes, I could tell he was slow. I could see he wanted to keep the fight close. He wanted to catch me and smother me with his fists or maybe with his arms, grabbing and crushing me with the pythons that hung from his shoulders.

For some reason, I had a sudden image of Hulk Hogan as "Thunderlips" walking forward, picking me up above his head, and tossing me into the crowd. I smiled and shook my head. My opponent grunted and scowled. I'm sure he thought I was laughing at him. His feet pounded on the canvas as he came after me with a new determination.

I bounced in place and watched him approach, trying to calculate his attack. He threw his left in a wide arching hook toward my head. I leaned my head back and bounced to my right. He turned toward me and I watched his right hand follow the same, yet opposite trajectory toward my head. I ducked and bounced and threw a straight left into his ear—THWAP. The contact caught us both off guard. He turned and threw a combination, left-right. I ducked with ease and caught him with two clean shots on the bridge of his nose—BOOP-BOOP.

Humm... again my voice echoed in my head. *Am I missing something?* I wondered how I landed my punches so easily. He stood in front of me, both fists touching his chin, he bounced a few times and tossed up another softball. I took a half step back, his fist glided by my face. "Strike three," I said in an audible voice and then stepped forward and landed three clean shots—right hook-left-left. He staggered back two steps, but I could see they didn't do much damage.

I followed him as he caught his balance and threw a fury into my midsection—left-right-left-right—over and over. Before I knew it he lifted both of his hands above his head and brought them down on the top of my skull with a force I had never felt before. I fell to my knees and another thud rang in my right ear. I dropped to my hands and instinctively reached for his legs. He reached down, grabbed me around my waist, and threw me to the side.

"Shit," I said as he barreled toward me. I stammered to my feet just in time to receive another blow to the face. And there it was, the adrenaline I'd been waiting for. It coursed through my body. I was tingling from head to toe. I couldn't tell if I was riding high or about ready to pass out. But I didn't care. I danced out of the way and blinked my eyes. I shook my head and took a deep breath. He looked at me puzzled and gave pursuit. He dove at me with both hands flying, looking for a knockout blow. I bobbed my head and moved. He turned and threw wild punches. I dropped and ran like a linebacker toward his legs, hitting him hard with my right shoulder, lifting his feet off the mat just enough to drive him into the cage. I felt his hands flailing above me trying to land fists on my back. They felt like love taps as the adrenaline masked any pain.

I lifted him again, just enough to turn him toward the center of the octagon and bring him down to the canvas. I ended up in a side mount and began thrusting my right fist repeatedly into the side of his face. He brought his arms up and tried to block my punches, but I pulled my fist high into the air and down squarely between his eyes. He brought his hands to his face. I switched between knees and fists—knees and fists. He tried to stop the onslaught, but I continued—

As we drove back to the farm, my head still reeling from the fight, the music blasted and my hosts serenaded me with a trio of off-key country ballads—not my usual style, but they were having fun and I was riding a fighter's high. We stopped off at a roadside bar and they treated me to a burger and a beer. I didn't tell them that I was not yet twenty-one and not really a beer drinker. I figured I'd enjoy everything while I could, not knowing how long it would last.

Cowboy hats and boots filled the dance floor and when line dancing broke out in the middle of the room Manuel grabbed my arm and pushed me into the middle of the scrum. My two other hosts sat at the bar laughing as I stumbled through an assortment of songs I'd never heard before. Two sweethearts sidled up beside me and helped me make less of a fool out of myself and by the end of the night I had almost forgotten where I was and why I was there.

Chapter Nineteen

The sun was beaming through my window the next morning. I never knew what time it was when my eyes first opened, as there was no clock in the room and my cell phone was still missing. I lay there for a moment switching between blurry pictures of last night's after-fight festivities and thoughts about my missing phone. I smiled as I thought about the brunette who eventually won me over and led me to a back room in the bar. And then I sat up with more pressing matters. I wanted to share my experiences with my parents, with John and Q. I wanted to tell them about the fight, about the money that lay deep underground, below a mansion in the middle of nowhere. I could feel my other self, the one who was thrust deep into the far recesses of my mind, struggling to find a way to contact my other life.

I threw my clothes on and walked downstairs—deserted, as usual. I walked outside and looked around. I jogged toward the barn, but found no one along the way. I jogged back to the house, passed it about a mile, and stopped. A faint buzz was audible off in the distance. I jogged toward the sound another half mile and saw a group of men standing around a car. The faint buzz was now a low rumble and the closer I got the rumble turned to a thundering growl. The hood of the car was open and two men were leaning over the engine.

The group gathered around a cream-colored Ford Mustang with a black hood and thick black stripes down each side. I wasn't much of a car guy, but I did have to admit it was gorgeous. The paint glistened in the morning sun and the thundering roar shook the ground.

My three hosts stood in the group of maybe ten men silently watching the two men adjusting the engine. "Give it some gas," one of the two men bending over the engine yelled. A roar echoed into the fields and beyond as if the car was claiming its dominance over the grasslands.

I stood next to Jorge and leaned toward him. He was transfixed, listening to the car purr. "So, what's this?" I asked, breaking his concentration.

"My man—" He looked at me and smiled. "You survived the night." He laughed, put his arms around my shoulders, and gazed at the car. "This here is the nicest car within a hundred miles." He extended a flat palm and waved it in front of the powerful beast.

"It is beautiful," I replied, not knowing what else to say.

"Yeah, it sure is." He tightened his grip around my shoulders and looked at me out of the corner of his eye. "I'm glad you're here—want you to meet our driver." He let go and walked toward the car. "Gio," he yelled over the din of the engine, "come here and meet our fighter." A svelte, well-built, young man, close to my age, stepped out of the car, wiped his hands on the front of his jeans, and sauntered over. "This here is Gio," he nodded toward the young man. "And this is the motherfucker who kicks people's asses," he nodded my direction. "Gio's our number one driver. He's racing this weekend. If you're not banged up from your next fight, you can go with us if you want."

"Yeah, okay—I'd like that." We stood for a moment, watching the two men fiddle with the engine. "So," I turned to Jorge, "am I able to get my phone back?" He didn't answer as he was once again engrossed in the throaty call of the "Big Horse" revving in front of the pack of men. I shook my head, started walking away, but turned back. "Hey, Gio," I called after the young driver, "maybe I'll see you this weekend." He nodded and waved.

"Yo, ass-kicker," Jorge called after me, "don't worry about the outside world," he said, raising his eyebrows and shaking his head. "That's not what you're here for... and I can't do anything about the phone anyway." He shrugged and turned back to the car.

I tilted my head and looked at him for a moment, and then jogged to the barn.

* * *

Music filled the barn as I slowly peddled an old stationary bike that I found hidden among a pile of ancient farm equipment in a storage room in the corner—another harken back to my dad's love for 80s rock. "Bang your head..." Quiet Riot brought me back to the early days of my life, playing with toys in the garage as my dad's favorite music reverberated from his boom box while he whittled away on one of his many projects.

My motivation to work that morning was less than usual. Normally, I would have some carryover from the fight the night before, some lasting, residual high from the pounding, the win, the energy of the crowd. But this was different. Maybe it was the three hours at the bar. Maybe it was because the energy from the crowd was much more subdued, the almost golf clap reaction to my demise of my opponent. But, most likely it was my fixation on my missing phone, not the actual phone itself, but the connection with the outside world and the other reality it represented. And the music didn't help—as it conjured up memories of my dad and stuck me right in the middle of my two realities, both sets of hands stretched out beside me as far as they could reach, one trying to hold on to the reality I was currently in, the other trying to grasp the one that had slipped away.

After a while, I got off the bike. I paced around the barn. My fingers began to tingle, but this time they weren't craving the fight. I was irritated and the adrenaline ran through my body, waking it up, alerting me that something wasn't right. My irritation started to grow—and then morph into discomfort— into an underlying feeling of regret. I felt the inevitability of my circumstances. I was stuck on this farm with no end in sight. I had a false sense of freedom. I could move around the farm. I could wake up and go to bed when I pleased. But I had no control. I couldn't leave. I couldn't contact my friends or family. I started to question my own decisions, the choices I made to follow the large man's instructions without question—to take the ticket—to walk through the airport—to wait for over an hour to board the flight—and then to board with a feeling of excitement. *What the fuck was I doing? How did I allow this to happen?* I paced. I questioned. I seethed.

I walked to the corner of the barn, to the heavy bag that hung from the rafters—THWACK. Dust flew into the air as my right hand made contact. THWACK—THWACK—THWACK. I stood back and watched the dust dance and then dissipate into shadowy beams of light that shone through the windows above.

I hopped on my toes and leaned in, throwing lefts and rights. The bag swung. I moved. I bounced. I punched.

I marched around the barn with a sense of malaise. I was lost in my own irritation, my own dismay. I was angry. I was scared. I was confused. My hands tingled. My heart pounded. And for some reason I stopped, but my heart wouldn't slow down. "Motherfucker," I yelled to the tattered ceiling. It hit me. I finally realized what had happened, why I let it happen— or really, why I wasn't able to prevent it from happening—to prevent myself from being lured into this underworld.

I sat in the rusty chair, rested my elbows on my knees and my face in my hands. I let myself calm down. I slowed my breathing. Yet, while I finally figured out what was going on inside me, what got me into this situation, I didn't allow the words to form in my mind. I couldn't open myself up to the truth. But I knew the answer was hovering with my other self, in my other reality. My other self was there, tucked away in my subconscious, waiting to reveal to my current self what had happened and what I had become.

Memories flooded my mind—sitting at dinner with my family—walking with my arm around Chan's shoulders, with pride, after filling our pockets with the loose change that had been hurled through the air at me after I demolished another poor soul on the field behind the apartments. I saw myself training, first in the gym with my club team, and then with my high school team. And finally, I felt my hand being raised as I won my last high school match and was crowned two-time state champion. All the hard work I had put in—all the discipline it took to accomplish that feat flashed through my head. And then I looked where I was and what I had become—a sideshow act for a faceless crowd of wealthy deviants, placing bets on the bodies of young men who had been ripped from their lives.

I felt ashamed. I was angry at myself. I should have been heading back to college, but instead, I got myself caught up in a life I didn't know how to escape. And it finally popped out. The truth was clear. I sat there, trying to block it out—trying to wish it away. But it hovered and slowly started to make its way from the background of my subconscious to the foreground of my current reality. It was as if my previous self was standing next to my current self, looking deep into his eyes. My previous self squinted and took a breath, yet didn't say a word. He walked over to my current self and put his arms around him. "It's okay," he told him. I felt my previous self comforting my current self. And then I felt the words quietly escape my lips—an audible whisper—"You're an addict." I sat there, allowing my previous self to embrace my current self, holding him in his arms, comforting him. "You'll be okay though—you're strong—you'll find a way out," my previous self reassured my current self.

That night, I lay in bed, staring at the ceiling, trying to make sense of my new discovery. *How can I be an addict?* My former self dropped the foreboding question. I lay quietly, trying to snuff out the answers, not wanting them to take shape. *I'm clean. I'm not an alcoholic. I don't take drugs.* I tried to convince myself everything was okay. I couldn't believe what I was asking myself and the answers that started to form. I pushed the questions from my thoughts—I avoided the answers. I couldn't come to terms with the reality taking shape in front of me, a reality that had actually taken shape long ago. *I was always on track. I was always driven towards my goals*, I thought, *but maybe there was another force controlling my actions.*

After tossing and turning for what seemed like hours, I

realized I wasn't clean. In fact, I did take drugs. Not only that, I was the manufacturer, the distributor, the dealer. Standing in front of my opponents, allowing them to pound me in the face, I was manufacturing the stimulants that my body craved, feeding my addiction. I pondered this thought, and as I did, my heart began to pound, my body started craving, my hands started tingling ever so slightly. The visceral desire flowed through my veins. I tried to subdue the urge, but it wasn't under my control.

I finally stopped fighting it and allowed myself to accept the reality. From the first time I was cracked in the face on the field behind the apartments—from the first time I looked into the mirror and smiled at the aftermath—I was addicted. I could trace the slow trajectory from the early days of addiction to the battles on the mat in my college room, trading blows with the teammate who kept me from the starting lineup. And then, like an addict trying to overtake his heightened tolerance to find that same high—that same buzz—I fell deeper into darkness. I was easily seduced by the large man. As easily as the addict embraces the crack pipe, I embraced the dark underbelly of illegal fighting. I repeatedly stepped into the ring knowing it would give me what my body craved, just as the addict wraps their lips around a pipe and fills their lungs.

I suddenly realized there was a darkened light shining through me, there always had been—a light which, instead of illuminating my path, sucked all the light around me into what had ultimately become a vortex. From the time I stuck a screwdriver into the socket and was blown back onto my diapered ass, the vortex had a hold on my desires. I now understood that this vortex was fueling the singularity I was once afraid would steal me away from my path and prevent me from becoming the person I was capable of becoming.

At that moment, lying in my darkened room, somewhere on a farm deep in the southern reaches of America, I had to figure a way out. So, I embraced my former self and allowed him to stand in tandem with my current self in my current reality as I knew they would need to work together to get me to a place where I had control. I needed my current self to fight in the deep underbelly of this noxious world and I knew I needed my former self to keep me sane and focused.

When I got up the next morning, it was life as usual, at least that's what I was determined to convince everyone around me. I jogged from field to field, warming my body and preparing for my morning workout. I waved to my three hosts, who stood by one of the many corn fields on the property. I made my way into the barn, found another throwback to days gone by, and listened as the music and the whiz of the treadmill filled the room.

Ninety minutes later I was back outside, letting the sweat drip down my back and slowly dissipate as my lungs filled with fresh air. I looked around. A flock of birds darted to and fro, filling the cloudless sky with life and motion, flowing one way and the next, reminding me of tides on the shores of the Pacific Ocean on a family vacation a few years past. I smiled as the memories warmed my heart and nostalgia filled my body. I used these feelings to fuel my desire to move forward. I worked at replacing the continued craving for stimulation with the desire to get back to my old life, my family, familiar places and times. My two selves stood, juxtaposed in my mind, the one, fearless and ready to fight, the other, sensible and focused on a way out.

Chapter Twenty

The cloudless sky fueled my morning run as I bounded to the far reaches of the farm. I ran to the entrance where I came and went on fight nights. I ran back, passed the house where I slept each night, all the way up the gravel drive, stopping at a large metal gate that bordered the property line. Outside the gate, a vacant road went both directions with no destination in sight. I finished my work out, lying in the middle of the cage in the middle of the barn, flat on my back, arms outstretched on the canvas, palms facing the rafters above, pools of sweat forming beneath my body. I spent time communicating with my two selves. I knew what I needed from each and I was learning to set one aside, close by, still in my mind's eye, while I embraced the other. Today I was the fighter and I allowed my former self to watch as I called upon the beast within to be prepared for whatever came my way that night. My former self watched, intently nodding as if he was enjoying the show.

Strangely, even though I was sure I was the fighter at the moment, I felt the calm and focus of my former self, almost as if my two realities began to morph together, each taking on needed aspects of the other. Once I was able to embrace the reality of my addiction, I gained more and more control over both sides, feeling as if they were now almost opposite sides of the same person.

When I left the barn, I had a few hours before my hosts whisked me away to my next fight, so I walked back to the house and made myself a chicken sandwich. I sat in the kitchen sipping on a Glacier White VitaWater and letting the chicken satisfy my stomach. I stood up and walked over to the window. I peered into the backyard and down to a distant corner of the farm I had yet to fully explore. I noticed a couple of outbuildings on a day of exploring a week or so ago and thought I would spend the next couple of hours checking them out. I felt I would go stir crazy if I had to stay here much longer—if walking around the corners of the wide-open acres was all there was to occupy my free time.

As I approached the first of the two buildings, I heard quiet chatter and peered into a large open barn door. Gio, the young driver I met just a few days ago, stood next to the cream-colored Mustang with a man wearing greasy coveralls. The barn was lit by three large fluorescent lights hanging from the rafters that extended across the open room. Car parts were strewn about the dirt floor and a slew of tools were sitting on a long workbench and hanging from a far wall.

Gio turned around and smiled while the man in the coveralls kept his head deep in the engine, the sound of tools clinking away.

"Hey—how's it going?" Gio greeted me with surprise.

"Good—it's going good." I returned his smile. "You must be getting ready for your race."

"Yeah—we just brought the car back from a test run," he said, as the man in the coveralls pulled his head from the engine, wiped his forehead with a handkerchief, and stuck his face back under the hood.

"How's it looking?"

"She ran well. Everything seems to be in place. The race has been postponed a few days, so we're in good shape," he patted the roof of the car. "Your next fight's tonight, isn't it?

"Supposed to be," I nodded, "but I'm never really in the loop. I just do what I'm told."

"Sounds familiar," he nodded his head and scrunched his eyes. "Well, good luck with the fight."

"Since your race isn't until next week, I may have had two more fights by then. If I'm still in one piece, I'll try to get there."

"If you do, make sure you get into the pit. I'm sure they'll bring you down if you want. There's no better feeling than the rush of the engine up close."

"Alright—I'll be sure to ask." I reached out and we shook. He held onto my hand for a moment and motioned with his head toward the car.

"Before you go, you want to sit behind the wheel?"

"Yeah, sure. That'd be cool."

He ran over to the tools on the wall, opened a drawer on the workbench, and pulled out a set of keys. "Here." He tossed them to me. "You know how to drive a stick?"

"Yeah—my dad taught me a few years ago in his little Honda 2000."

"Good—but this beast has quite a bit more power. It takes a lot to control her." He let out a breathy laugh. "Start her up and put her in neutral. When I give you the signal, rev her up a few times."

I sat in the drivers seat, the cool, smooth leather cradling my body, and then turned the key. The car came to life with a deep, vibrating hum that shook the cockpit. Gio pounded the top of the car. I pumped my foot several times. The roar of the engine cascaded up and then down—up and then down. I held my foot down halfway—it revved to a crescendo, hit its peak, and slowed to a purr. The engine idled as I relaxed behind the wheel. I turned the key again and listened to the reverberations bounce around the room and disappear.

Gio poked his head in the window, "Nothing like it, huh?"

"Whew—got that right," I replied, my body still shaking.

"That's mother-fucken-power," he laughed, opening the door to let me out. "Hope to see you at the race."

"I'll see if my body's feeling up to it," I smirked. "I've never been before."

"Well, it'd be nice to see yuh. Not many folks my age around here."

"How long you been here? "

"A few months, but I'm not sure exactly—you?"

"A few weeks." I handed him the keys. "You stay on the farm?'

"Nah-I'm in a house a couple miles out."

I gave him a curious look. "Well, good luck with the race. Not sure if I'll see you or not." We pounded fists.

He seemed like he was going to ask me something, but instead cleared his throat, "Good luck to you, too." He folded his arms and smiled.

By the time I got back to the house, a group had gathered out front. Jorge stood in the center, hands raised in the air, shouting incoherently. The men surrounding him were clearly farm workers, gloved hands, dirty denim jeans, boots, and either a beat-up baseball cap or cowboy hat covering their heads.

I walked past them, not quite curious enough to figure out what they were doing, and headed inside. I gathered a couple drinks and a few protein bars from the kitchen, went upstairs, and loaded them in my backpack. I picked up the duffle bag on the floor and set it on the bed beside me. I unzipped it and stared at the stacks of hundred-dollar bills I was yet to count. I knew what deviance the money represented and wondered how full it would be before I found a way out of this place.

I thought back to my first paid fights. What a difference—from the unofficial scraps on the field behind the apartments, where Chan and I pocketed loose change thrown by kids my own age, to the drunken cheers of blue-collar workers and a few hundred dollars. Now, I was pulling in hundreds of thousands in the basement of some nameless mansion, under the gaze of one-percenters who barely paid attention to the violence taking place under the chandelier in the center of the room.

I zipped up the duffle and shoved it under the bed. Staring out the window, I was hoping tonight would mark the end of this chapter of my life. The sun still lingered behind the distant hills. I lay back, closed my eyes, and felt the calm of darkness overtake me.

* * *

Stepping onto the white marbled floor, I had a strong sense of my two selves standing side by side, guiding me in tandem. I felt more in control of myself than I had for a long time. My former self was sitting calmly watching as my current self paced back and forth, focusing on the night's confrontation. Led by my three hosts, I made my way through the maze of hallways, down the stairs, and back to the underground fight lair that housed unlimited pockets of money, alcohol, and gambling. I was surprised to see the room was full, people were already dining and a fight was well underway.

While warming up in my private room, I was visited by the men in the gray and blue jackets, although this time they were both wearing black tuxedos. "Looking forward to your fight tonight," the man in the gray jacket walked toward me. I stood in place—no reaction. "Your fight was moved later in the card this time. People enjoyed watching you." He looked at me as if he expected me to reply, but I didn't. "You're the fourth fight of the night. They'll be expecting even more out of you this time." I hopped from foot to foot and gave him a quick nod.

"We have faith in you," the man in the blue jacket added as he looked me straight in the eye and patted me on the shoulder. "We'll see you after the fight," he said as they left the room.

I threw a few quick jabs into the air, squatted down, and carried out my ritual wrestler's warm-up. While many of these tactics were not useful in these unscripted fights, I was a wrestler and always would be. The familiar movements got my body going, my heart pounding.

The door opened and my cornerman from the last fight joined me. He looked at me with a grin. "Doesn't look like you need much from me right now. You seem to have everything under control." He grabbed a roll of tape and wrapped my hands in silence. When he was done he looked at me cockeyed and then shook his head. "Not sure where these guys found you, but you're fun to watch." He paused for a moment. "Give us a good show tonight, people are looking forward to seeing you out there again." He left.

I sat down and closed my eyes. I relaxed my body and mind. I felt different. The control I had over my alter egos lent an abnormal feeling of calm to my preparations, almost as if I had to tell myself to wake up. I was used to the tingling hands, the adrenaline coursing through my body. I cautioned myself not to let my guard down. I had to fight like I always did, but at that point, I was missing the normal edge I had before my previous fights. I nodded my head and rocked forward and back rhythmically, "Okay," I told myself out loud, "that's fine. I've been here before."

My cornerman popped back in with an excited flair. "Knock-out, my man. You're up." He held the door open as I rose to my feet, rolled my neck, hopped up and down a few times, then headed out. He followed me and my three hosts joined in the walk through the maze of tables, falling in like bodyguards. I leapt up the stairs and into the cage. My opponent was waiting for me impatiently, pacing back and forth on the far side of the canvas. *Hmmm*, I said knowingly to myself. *He's a fucken wrestler*—I could tell instantly—*this ought to be interesting.*

The announcer introduced the fighters, his voice reverberating around the muted room. I didn't recognize my opponent's name, but did notice the abnormal number of consonants in his last name and the -s-k-y- ending. *He's gotta be from Eastern Europe*, I told myself with a warning. And all of a sudden, the tingle appeared and moved from my fingertips, into my hands and up my arms. I told myself to focus, to fight like a beast, but to stay within myself. His thick cauliflower ears and flattened nose told me everything I needed to know. This was going to take everything I had.

We walked to the center of the ring, listened to whatever rules the referee claimed there were, and touched fists. We took a few steps back... and the fight commenced.

We slowly made our way forward and began to circle to our left, hands in front of our faces. He stopped and bounced from foot to foot, then paced back and forth in front of me. I mirrored his movements. He was quick and agile, but I sensed a chink in his armor, a restlessness that could play to my advantage, although I figured, with his background, he would mitigate much, if not all, of my advantage—and I was sure he had the same feeling about me.

A minute into the bout, it was eerily quiet in the marbled room. The echo of the roulette table bounced off the walls and the clinking of tableware floated over plates of caviar, veal, and lobster that was being eaten daintily by the seated onlookers, napkins placed just so on their laps. If this were any of my previous fights in one of the dingy warehouses, the crowd would be audibly restless at this point. I figured the frustration of this noble crowd was felt in the betting circle, no one sitting at the dining tables around the cage would break character. There was a certain decorum expected and therefore followed. They were watchers of a Greek tragedy, sitting with their opera glasses held in white-gloved hands.

He stopped and pounded his fists together. I bounced in place. He took a step toward me and feigned a leg kick. I took a step back. And suddenly he rushed me, pushed me with two hands in the chest, and threw punches at my face. I bobbed my head in time, but felt the wind of his clenched fists breeze by the side of my face.

He threw two more punches—WHIT—WHIT. I moved to the side and pulled my hands in front of my face. The second punch landed on my right forearm. He was quicker than any of my previous opponents. WHIT—WHIT—THUD. He landed a solid jab to my right ear. I bounced back two steps. He lowered his level and shot for my legs. A bit surprised, I sprawled my legs back, but my feet hit the cage behind me. I stopped his shot just enough, but he drove forward, grabbed around my legs, and shoved me against the chain link.

We struggled there for a moment before he tried to lift me up. I thrust my hips in and brought an elbow down between his shoulder blades. He drove me against the fence. I pressured into him and freed my right leg and then immediately pushed down on his head with both hands and quickly brought my knee up, landing it squarely on his face.

He let go, retreated a few steps back, regained his balance, and bounced in place. I followed him forward, cautiously pursuing him as he began circling. I could feel my former self step to the forefront and join my current self. Suddenly, I felt a new clarity. I wasn't driven by pure adrenaline anymore. I started thinking of it like a chess match, looking for ways to counter his movements and set up my attack.

As he bounced one way and then the other, I circled toward him and started cutting off angles, dictating his movements with mine, trying to trap him against the chain link barrier that separated us from the well-mannered crowd. He bounced, threw punches, and bounced again, trying to find a way to attack or circle out of danger.

THWAP—I threw my first punch of the fight, catching him off guard and landing it on his cheek. He ducked and bobbed his head. I timed my next two shots, missing the first, but landing the second on the bridge of his nose. We exchanged punches with a flurry, back and forth. I moved closer and shoved my forearms into his chest, trapping him on the fence. I brought my knees into his midsection, one after the other, but they were ineffective as he raised his legs and blocked much of the impact. We were stuck, grappling against the wall of the octagon. I threw punches and then knees. He blocked them successfully.

I heard my former self talking to my current self. He told him to take control. "This is your world," he told him. "I will be here for you when you need me. Do what you need to do." My current self stepped forward with a crooked grin, nodded his head, and awakened to the moment.

I let go of my opponent and stepped back to the center of the cage. I waved at him and pointed to the ground, encouraging him to step forward and meet me toe to toe. He shook his head and grunted in anger, then nodded and raised his fists. He bounced three times and marched forward with a determined step.

We stalked each other in a quick circle, one way and then the next. He landed a front kick to my midsection and attempted another—I sat my hips back and parried his leg to the side, stepped forward, and landed a jab-hook combination. We traded blows and kicks in the middle of the cage, neither of us backing down. I felt a trickle of blood seeping from my nose. The tingling in my body intensified as I let my current self fully embrace the fight.

He landed a solid shot to my left eye socket. I felt a rush of adrenaline and a smile crept onto my face. I dropped my hands below my chin and allowed him to connect two more clean shots. My heart pounded. My blood raced. I moved forward and fought through an onslaught of lefts and rights, raising my forearms in front of my body, and returning blows in his belly—THUD—WACK—THUD—THUD.

The exchange continued. He hit me with two solid low kicks. I felt the sting on the outside of my calf. I hopped, moved, and threw a left, then a right, grazing his face. He retaliated and sent me back a few steps with a quick combination. I regained my balance and stormed forward. He caught me with a roundhouse to my ribs, knocking me to the side. I squared up and barreled forward. We were forehead to forehead, exchanging punches.

163

And then I dropped down and shot for his legs. He sprawled, but I ran my feet and got my hips underneath me just enough to drive him to the canvas with a thud. He grunted as my right shoulder landed in his belly. He quickly squirmed into his guard and wrapped his legs around me. He peppered my sides with quick, little shots. I shoved my left forearm under his chin and hammered down into his face with the outside of my right fist. We grappled and fought. I continued hitting him in the face. He tried to block my punches. And then I was grabbed and pulled to my feet. My opponent got to his knees and took a deep breath. I thought the fight was over, but we were told to continue fighting. I looked around to see what was going on while my opponent slowly got to his feet. *Where was this in the fucken rules?* I scoffed to myself. And then quickly re-engaged.

He was ready and clocked me with a combination of kicks to my shin and ribs. I charged him like a rhino, not quite sure what I was doing. We collided and he stumbled back. I closed in and threw punch after punch—WHAP-WHAP-whiff-WHAP—landing and missing, landing and missing. I caught him cleanly under his left ear with a winding hook. His legs buckled, but he caught his balance. I threw a jab and missed. I landed a right-left, THUMP-THUMP. He fell to his butt and recovered into a sitting position.

He egged me on, trying to get me to attack him into his guard. I bobbed around, reached my hand out several times, attempting to grab a wrist or ankle. Finally, I squatted down and secured his right ankle. I pushed him in his chest with my right hand, and passed my right knee through, securing a side mount. I threw forearms and hammerfists to his face—and a couple knees to his side. He was absorbing the punishment with his hands and forearms. I kept them coming and he kept blocking.

I stopped the punches and leapt on top to a full mount. I leaned on his chest with both forearms and worked to control his wrists. We grappled around until I finally had control—and then I let it fly. I sat over him and threw punches, one after the other—one after the other. He tried to move his head and bring his hands in front of his face, but he could no longer keep up with my onslaught and finally, his hands went limp and fell to his side. I sat in the guard for a moment and looked into his closed eyes, blood was splattered all over his face and was dripping from his nose and mouth. I looked around. Nobody came to stop the fight. The referee stood near, but showed no urgency to do anything.

I got off, and then squatted next to him. He was breathing deep heavy breaths, his chest was visibly rising—and falling. A doctor came and leaned over him. My name boomed over the loudspeaker. A muted golf clap floated in the darkened room, barely enough energy to penetrate the chain link walls of the cage. I raised my hands briefly, but the lack of emotion from the crowd was disappointing, so I dropped my arms and left the cage. By the time I weaved my way through the tables, to the locker room, all attention was back to the stock market, investments, and the upcoming classical dressage competition while they waited for the final fight.

A few minutes later, I was leaning against the wall with my head under the shower head. I could feel a pounding in my face where punches had landed as water ran from the top of my head down the back of my neck, over my back and torso, to the floor of the shower, and down the drain. I watched as the water started with a pinkish hue and quickly dissipated to clear. I took a deep breath and squatted down as the water continued to cover my body and relax my muscles. I stood up, reached to the handle on the wall, and listened to the squeak echo off the tiles as I turned it a half dozen times. The water dripped and then stopped, and then I stepped out of the shower.

I wrapped a towel around my waist and walked into the changing room where a man and woman were sitting silently. It was strange, but by this time, nothing was a surprise. The man smiled and nodded his head. I stood for a moment, perplexed, then returned his nod. I walked over to my backpack on the other side of the room, dropped my towel, rifled through my belongings, and pulled out my clothes. I dressed as the two individuals watched me quietly from their viewing gallery, then I sat and pulled on my socks and shoes.

I leaned back in my chair and looked at the couple. I crossed my right leg over my left and sat without a word. I had been in this world just long enough to know that there could be twists and turns at any moment, so I sat and waited for the surprise. The man finally introduced himself as a manager of fighters and wrapped his arm around the woman's shoulders, "This is my assistant," he paused, tilted his head, and then, as if an afterthought, told me her name. She leaned her half-naked body against his. I laughed to myself and nodded, *Yeah, right, assistant.* I stood up, aware another turn of events was hidden in plain sight and began packing my backpack. "I watched your two fights." He looked at me intently. "I've been impressed." And then he sat, head tilted, deep in thought. "I've been talking to..." he named the men in the gray and blue jackets. "I wanted to make sure we got a chance to meet." He looked at me out of the corner of his eye as he shared his attention with his half-dressed assistant. "I see a bright future for you."

"Are you going to purchase my rights?" I asked, adding air

quotes and a bit of sarcasm.

The man laughed. "I'm not sure what you mean. I'm going to watch you win this tournament and then hopefully you'll be open to talking about your future."

I nodded and raised my eyebrows. "Well, I'm not even sure what I'm doing here. I'll finish whatever fights they give me and then figure out what's next."

"Just so you're clear, I'm here to help you go legit. You're above this racket." He stood up and then offered his hand to the woman beside him. She stood up and leaned her body toward his as they eyed me up and down. "Keep your focus here and finish strong. I'll find you when it's all said and done." We shook hands and they walked out.

I gathered my belongings and headed home with my hosts, not giving the encounter a second thought.

Chapter Twenty-One

Three days later, I was lying in the middle of the octagon in the barn letting the sweat pool on the canvas around me, my chest moving up and down as my heart slowed. The boombox blared a more contemporary rock ballad than usual. I listened as I fell deep into relaxation and visualized myself bouncing around, landing punches, and taking a faceless opponent down with a thud.

I twisted my body this way and that, stretching my back, and then sat up and leaned forward over straight legs, feeling the muscles stretch behind my knees.

The music ended as I grabbed my backpack and walked out into the soft breeze. The sun beat down hard as usual. I walked to a small line of trees that I found recently, sat down, leaned against one of the larger trunks, and pulled out a bottled water from my bag. I didn't want to admit to myself how nice it was on the farm. I had no worries. I lived the life of a fighter with everything I really needed, except for maybe a training partner and a coach—and contact with the outside world. But I quickly brought myself back to reality. No matter how nice it was relaxing under the canopy of the mature trees that lined one of the many fields that harbored my existence, I had to keep perspective.

I sipped the water and watched a tractor rumble slowly by, pulling a flatbed full of farmhands who looked worn out. I assumed they were headed for lunch down the way as it was just past noon. I turned my head and followed it with my eyes as it continued down the path and disappeared behind a field of corn stalks.

I closed my eyes and listened. An occasional bird or the buzzing of a bee would methodically creep into the quiet stillness. If I were here under normal circumstances I would be relaxed, I would be enjoying myself, but there was no letting my guard down. I was still running ideas through my head—*how would I get away? Could I find my escape at the next fight? Was there some discrete way of disappearing into the night and vanishing without a trace?* And suddenly, I was reminded of a short story I read in high school about a man who was stuck on an island only to find out he was being hunted like a wild animal by a rich aristocrat. I vaguely remembered the protagonist defeating the hunter in the end. But I also remembered the ending left unanswered questions and I didn't want unanswered questions in my story. I had to take control somehow before it was too late—if it wasn't already too late.

I spent the next day and a half working out and running the same ideas through my head until I found myself face-to-face with my third opponent. He was a tall, rangy, less than inspiring-looking fighter, although he did remind me of Royce Gracie, the dangerously lethal Brazilian Jiu-Jitsu fighter who stormed the UFC in its infancy. *Shit, what if this guy's his relative? What if he's a Gracie protege?* The thoughts rattled around my head until the bell rang and my opponent charged straight forward and shot at my legs. I sprawled and we scrambled around the ground, in and out of the guard. I was on top for a moment. He started hitting my lower back and kidney with his right heel. I reached my left arm around his leg to stop the pounding. He reached his arms around my head and pulled my head tight to his chest, then used his right hand to land punches to the side of my face.

Even though I was on top, my right arm was stuck between our two bodies, and I was being controlled by his guard. I was trying to stay calm while I figured out what to do, but I wasn't used to the sudden feeling of helplessness. My first goal was to keep my arms close to my body, safe from unknown locks that would cause me to tap out. I closed my eyes and slowed my breathing. He kept my head tight to his chest, his legs wrapped around my torso.

I wriggled my upper body back and forth slightly, working to free my right arm. I managed to pull it in and keep it close to my side—my left arm, still cradling his right leg. It was a slow but excruciating start. His fist continued its attack on my left ear and cheek. I could feel the side of my face throb more with each punch. I worked my right arm in between his arm and my head and was able to create space. I landed a few blows of my own which slowed down his incessant pounding. And then I broke free from his guard just enough to squat over him and catch both of his lower legs with my arms. He squirmed, trying to free his legs and kick me. I dropped his legs and backed off.

He stood up. We circled and bounced. He stepped forward several times and attacked with a front kick each time, but I was out of reach. He circled with a roundhouse. I leaned back and his foot whiffed by my face. He threw another front kick and I caught it with my left arm. I leaned to my left and delivered a sidekick, something I had never done in a fight, but had practiced numerous times on the heavy bag back home and on the farm. It landed, but with little impact.

I kept his leg locked under my armpit and brought my free arm over and lifted his caught leg high into the air, placing it on my shoulder and running him backward into the cage. I circled him toward the center of the ring and swept his leg. I fell awkwardly on top of him, but managed to fight for a side mount and instantly brought my fist into his cheekbone several times. He flailed his arms in defense trying to find a way to stop my assault. I landed punch after punch to the side of his head and then brought my hand up and straight down on his nose. He was helpless—for the moment—yet, somehow he was able to catch my wrist.

We struggled there, his face bleeding, my face throbbing. I took the moment to slowly maneuver for position and catch my breath. My normal avalanche of punches was not as effective against his defense. I tightened my grip, kept my chin and forehead low, and felt around for a new hold. Somehow I was able to free my wrist, slip my left arm under his head, and grab his far arm, catching a reverse half. He suddenly popped his hips up and turned away. I lowered my chin into his chest and held him there, but a moment later, he slipped out of my grasp.

Just as he tried to turn and face me, I sprang forward and caught him on his belly. I let him scramble to his knees and threw my right leg and then my left leg around him. He pulled his arms into his body and tucked into a tight ball. I wrapped my right arm around his face and grabbed his far shoulder. He rolled around and kicked his legs trying to get free before I secured a hold. I wrapped my left arm around and onto his head. He slowed his movement as I applied pressure on top of his head and across his throat. He collapsed to his side and tried to slip his hand between my arms. He struggled there for a moment, trying to free himself from my lock, but soon brought his left hand up and tapped three times.

Like before, no one came to stop the match, and I felt I was drawn back in time. I was that little boy on the field behind the apartments with none of the bigger kids around to keep us safe. I was competitor and referee. I had control and needed to figure out how to bring the match to its conclusion. The difference was, I wasn't a little kid on the field behind the apartments, and the stakes were much higher. I could see this coming to a sorry end. *Was this a fight to the death? If I let him up, would the fight continue?*

I loosened my grip, sunk my arms deeper, and squeezed harder. He wheezed—a muffled cough followed. He reached out and tapped a second time. But again, no stoppage came. I was at a loss. What was next? Choke him until he passed out—for good?

I glanced to the side—one way and then the next. No movement from anyone outside of the two in the center of the cage and we were embroiled in a conflict that might only end one way.

I relaxed one more time, but kept my grip. I tightened just enough to let him know I was still in control. He didn't react, but his eyes were open and focused and his chest was heaving up and down. I wasn't sure how much time had passed, but I was now getting angry.

I took a deep breath and felt my current self take a step backward in my mind. My former self stepped forward, taking complete control as my current self watched. I released my grip and raised my body, standing tall under the chandelier that cast its light upon us. I looked down on my opponent, who lay there awake but beleaguered.

I heard a restless murmur from the crowd—no beer bottles thrown—no profanity—just uneasy banter. I could tell they were not pleased. They wanted me to finish him off. I was waiting for the call from the crowd—waiting to be crowned the merciful gladiator—but this was not a Hollywood script.

I looked around, extended my hands out wide, and circled the octagon. Still no reaction from the referee, who stood off to the side watching, no acknowledgment from the affluent onlookers, clad in Armani and Couture, their polished elegance contrasting the raw violence they barely acknowledged in the center of the room. I walked to the gate and rattled it several times. It was locked. I pounded my fist against the chain link, then hopped up and sat high on the top of the cage wall, towering above the crowd. I looked around, grunted at the ceiling, and sat for a moment—then swung my legs over and climbed down, out into the mass of dinner tables, silent watchers eyeing me intently.

By the time I was halfway through the winding trail of lobster and caviar, all eyes were fixated on me. The roulette tables were still. The clinking of silverware and glasses could be heard no more.

I disappeared into my dressing room and sat on a chair. My heart was surprisingly steady. I let my body relax as I wondered what my next move should be. *Did I play it off as usual, shower up, and follow my three hosts through the underground fight ring and back to the surface? Are people even going to care what I do?* I didn't know. What I did know was my control over myself was growing stronger. I knew I wasn't in control of everything, but at least I felt in control of myself—my decisions—my conscious—my subconscious—my two selves.

I stood up, paced around the room, and hopped in place. I

released whatever tension remained in my body. I walked in circles. I took deep breaths. I sat on the floor and bent my body this way and that, stretching my back and my legs and my neck and my arms. I lay back and closed my eyes. I was finally myself again. I was finally ready to move forward. I wasn't quite sure how, but I knew it was time.

When I left the dressing room, twenty minutes later, the final fight of the night was well underway, but no one was paying attention as I was swarmed by a mob of gold and silver—of glittering watches and cuff buttons and diamond rings. They wanted my picture. They wanted my autograph. They wanted to touch me. They wanted to take me home. Money flew through the air, wads of hundred-dollar bills landed at my feet. I felt hands on my body accosting me, rubbing me, touching me.

I was out of sorts. I was caught in a nightmare. Here I had convinced myself I had a semblance of control. But I was thrust deep into a third reality. I was not my own man anymore. I tried to look around and find my hosts. I tried to fight my way through the crowd in the direction I thought was my escape.

I finally made it to the edge of the room near the door that led the way out. I was panting. My heart was pounding. I scampered up the stairs, through the maze of hallways, onto the white marble floor, and threw the front door. I ran into the driveway and stopped.

* * *

Later that night, I lay in my dark room, on a silent night on the farm, a far cry from the mob in the hidden underground below a nameless mansion in the middle of nowhere. I was saved by my three hosts who drove up moments later, as I stood at the end of the long circular drive. The music was blaring as always and there was no mention of the frivolities or the fight. They sang. They yelled over one another. They laughed. And soon, we were back on the farm.

I didn't know what to think as I closed my eyes and ran the night through my mind. I was glad I made it out in one piece, although I was actually a little miffed at myself for not filling my pocket with the wads of money thrown at my feet. And then I laughed to myself... *it's a long way from the loose change on the field behind the apartments.*

Chapter Twenty-Two

I woke to the man in the gray jacket sitting in a chair on the other side of the room. He had a brown paper bag in one hand and a cup of coffee in the other. I sat up halfway and leaned on my elbow. "You created quite a stir last night," he said with a sideways grin. I shrugged. "You're the talk of the town—" he looked at me for a moment, then added "—everyone wants to know your story." He held the paper bag toward me. "You left this behind." I sat on the edge of the bed and grabbed the bag. "And I added your winnings." I opened it and peered in. The bag was full of wads of money from the night before and two large envelopes. "I've never seen anything quite like it," he smiled derisively, "the stunt you pulled," he shook his head, "climbing out of the cage." He laughed breathlessly. "You've definitely got balls."

He stood up, walked to the door, and stopped. He turned, then paused as if deep in thought. "I want you to go to the race with me today. You deserve the day off and you need to meet a few people."

"I can use some ice and some ibuprofen, first."

"I'll do you one better. I'll take you out to breakfast and then we'll stop by my masseuse on the way. She does wonders."

Two hours later I was walking out of Sarina's massage parlor.

I knew it was sketchy from the start when I was driven to a back alley in a black SUV with tinted windows, sitting in the back seat between two muscle-bound men. I got out and was directed to walk through an unmarked door into a dark, incense-filled lobby. I was led to one of several hidden rooms in the back by a slight, scantily clad young woman. Even though it was not the athletic massage I was hoping for, I climbed back into the SUV, smelling of rubbing oils and feeling more relaxed.

We arrived at the race track down a long, tree-lined road that led through the complex of parking lots and wide open fields, finally pulling into a covered parking garage behind the grandstands overlooking the track. We walked into the sun, went through a security checkpoint, and found Gio and his team of mechanics making last-minute adjustments to the cream-colored Mustang. The races were due to start at noon. It was just after eleven and they were busily preparing for the race, so I followed the man in the gray jacket as he shook hands with mysterious men in suits and sunglasses. I stood back a few feet, accompanied by his two henchmen. They stood on either side of me, hands clasped behind their backs.

We walked from pit to pit. It was evident he had made these rounds many times—handshakes and personal greetings, a few sarcastic barbs and challenges for the day's races strewn about. We ran into the man in the blue jacket standing next to two gentlemen, deep in conversation. One man, with powdery gray hair, was waving his hands and laughing. The other, wearing dark slacks and a black and red team jacket was listening intently, arms folded, head tilted to the side.

The man in the blue jacket turned and smiled. He shook hands with the man in the gray jacket and turned to me with open arms. "Here he is," he bellowed joyfully. "I was just talking about you." He placed the palm of his right hand on the center of my back and led me to the two men. "This is the young man I've been telling you about." He patted me on the shoulder. The two men stuck their hands out one at a time. I shook them in turn.

"Sounds like you had quite a fight last night," the gray-haired man said.

"It was something, all right," I replied matter-of-factly.

"I was just telling them about how they mobbed you when you left," the man in the blue jacket said. They normally don't show much emotion toward the fighters, but you got their attention," he added, shaking his head for emphasis.

They looked at me as if they were expecting a reply, maybe a little anecdote about the fight or a peek inside my fighter's mind, but I didn't want to give them the satisfaction. I wanted to stay in control of the only thing I had left. "It sure was different. Caught me off guard," keeping my reply simple and mysterious.

"We'll have to come to your next fight." The man in the team jacket added. "Haven't been in a long time."

"Well, it'll be worth it," the man in the gray jacket put his arm around my shoulder. "Sorry guys, I have to introduce him to the boss before the races begin." They nodded with understanding and turned back to their previous conversation.

I wondered who the boss was. I thought the men in the gray and blue jackets were the boss. I was curious, but also a bit scared. I worried that the deeper this went the harder it would be to get out. But I wouldn't have to wonder much longer as we entered a suite overlooking the track. There were three rows of lush seats facing a gigantic window at the front, a bar and tables full of food at the rear. People were mingling about, eating, drinking beer and wine.

A heavyset man in a navy polo shirt and slacks stood next to the bar holding a glass of red wine. I followed the man in the gray jacket as he navigated his way around a group of people and approached the heavyset man. He greeted the heavyset man with more formality than anyone else, then brought me forward. He told him I was the fighter "who was doing us proud."

The heavyset man nodded my direction. "Nice shiner," he grumbled in a deep voice. "Sounds like the other guy looks even worse." He took a drink from the wine glass in his hand and set it down. "I've been wanting to meet you," he continued. "When this little tournament you're in is over, you'll have to come see me. I've got plans for you."

It was never officially explained to me, nothing ever was, but from the formality exchanged, I gathered the heavyset man was the boss. *What next?* I wondered as I looked around the suite.

"You guys are welcome to watch the races from up here if you'd like. Got enough food and drink to satisfy a herd of elephants."

"Thanks. We'll be sure to enjoy ourselves," the man in the gray jacket replied, half nodding, half bowing in respect.

As I walked around the buffet table filling my plate, I was struck by the lavishness of the setup. The juxtaposition of the catered feast with the blue-collar draft beers in the grandstands created an irony I had never experienced before. I was sure the whole thing had been paid for by some sort of illegal enterprise, yet it was hard to deny how enticing it was.

I ate my fill of shrimp and small cubes of Kobe beef covered in some sort of brown sauce while we sat and watched the first few rounds of drags. Gio's reaction time was amazing. He was off the line and almost a complete car length ahead in his first two races. His first time was 7.75 seconds for ⅛ of a mile and the second was 7.59.

After the second race, the man in the gray jacket leaned over to me, "We found him in a small town across the border racing a beat-up Chevelle. He never won a race, but we could see his potential. He just needed the right team behind him."

So, he's just like me, I thought to myself. *Ripped from his previous life.* I stood up and leaned my forehead on the window and tried to find him in the throng of people near the track. I wondered if he was thinking about an escape plan, too.

Two hours later, we were watching the finals from the pit next to the track. It was totally different than watching from the suite. While the windows in the suite rattled and the seats moved as if by a small earthquake, being right next to the track was total immersion—a visceral experience. The rumbling shook the ground and enveloped my body. It was thrilling.

After the finals, Gio posed by his cream-colored Mustang and walked around the pit showing off his championship trophy. We talked for a little while, and I tried to find out a bit more about him. I soon realized we weren't the same at all. His decision was easy. The day a man in a suit approached him on the edge of a dirt track and handed him more money than he could possibly earn in two lifetimes he was gone. It was not difficult for him to leave a life of gang violence and poverty to cross the border for a chance at the American dream. I saw the appeal, a life filled with excitement—with money—with promise. In fact, I had to fight my desire to live this same life. I was experiencing things I had never experienced before and I had a bag full of money—most likely hundreds of thousands of dollars—sitting under the bed I slept in every night. So I never asked him about his escape plan.

Chapter Twenty-Three

Life continued as normal, at least normal for this reality. I spent the next two days working out and running around the farm. I made sure to jog past the barn where I found Gio and the mechanic working on his car not long ago. I wanted to know more about him. I wanted to have someone to talk to. But nobody was ever there, just a car under a blue tarp, resting in silence. I ran to all corners of the farm, with the off chance I would run into Gio. But I had no such luck.

Just after four a.m. the next morning, the day of my next fight, I heard a ruckus outside the house. I walked out to the porch and saw a dozen people hurriedly filling two big vehicles with boxes.

"What the fuck you standing there for?" Jefferson, my one host who had never said a word to me up until that point, belted at me. "The feds are on their way. We gotta get the fuck out."

I stood on the porch stunned, not quite understanding what he was saying. And then it hit me—they were screwed—I was screwed. *Holy shit. Do I want to go with them? Do I wait for the feds to show up?* Without really thinking, I ran upstairs and threw my belongings into my backpack and grabbed my duffel bag full of money from under the bed. I heard the vehicles outside roar to life and speed off. I ran downstairs clutching my two bags and then ran out the back door. I didn't know where to go.

I stood behind the house and looked around. The top of the sun was visible off in the distance. Just enough light peaked over the hills to see the outlines of trees and outbuildings—and there it was—exactly what I needed.

I secured my backpack over my shoulders and threw the strap of my duffle across my chest. I ran as best I could as the bags bumped against my body. Sirens echoed across the darkened sky. I picked up the pace and was soon at my destination. I grabbed the handle on the weathered barn door and attempted to open it, but it was locked. I ran around the other side of the barn and the one small door was barred shut. I picked up a large rock and tossed it through a window and threw my bags inside and then climbed up and over, cutting my hand on the broken glass. I fell to the ground. It was dark, but I knew what I needed was here. I got up and felt my way to the center of the room, hands out in front of me until both palms ran into a hard object. I grabbed the fabric and pulled, the tarp swooshed across the metal and fell to the ground. I felt for the handle, grabbed, and pushed the latch. The door opened. The dome light illuminated inside.

I turned and walked quickly to the other side of the barn, feeling my way with my feet and hands. I found my way to the workbench and pulled open a drawer, and then another, until I found several sets of keys. I grabbed them all and headed back to the dim light in the distance. I jumped in the car and searched in my hand until I found the right key. I inserted it into the ignition, but was afraid the roaring engine would attract too much attention. I knew this was my only chance at escape, so I turned on the headlights, got out of the car, unlatched the barn door, and pulled it open. I hustled back to the car, turned the key, and the beast rumbled to life.

"Fuck," I yelled to myself and I jumped out of the car, fumbled for my bags, and threw them in the front seat.

I sat down, shifted into first gear and pressed on the gas. The car burst into action, lurching forward and smashing into the edge of the open door. I tried to gain control of the steering wheel as the car careened forward into the wakening light. The only way I knew I might be safe was to make it to the far end of the farm where I discovered the back gate on one of my daily runs. So, I awkwardly guided the beast to the left, hit a bump, and leapt onto the gravel drive that led from one end of the property to the other. I looked in the rearview mirror. Total darkness. No one was following me.

I shifted from second to third and heard the engine's deep whine. Finally, the eyes of the beast illuminated the gate less than a hundred feet away. I didn't have time to get out and open it. I downshifted, hit the gas, and shifted back to third. The car collided with the metal gate and it exploded open and flung to the side on its broken hinges. The car bounced on uneven ground as I tried to find my way to the road. And then, up ahead, the unkempt road intersected a thoroughfare. I didn't know where it led, but it had to lead away from the farm.

The car was speeding, bouncing, shaking as I kept my foot heavy. I watched closely as the car bounded forward toward the paved road. I tried to time a quick turn at the right moment... I downshifted and turned the wheel to the left as hard as I could. The rubber burned and squealed into the vacant morning. I turned back to the right as the car fishtailed out of control. I swerved one way and then the other, finally gaining enough control to keep on the road. I didn't know where I was headed, but at that point, I didn't care, as long as it was away—far away—from the farm.

I looked at the speedometer. I was going over a hundred miles an hour. And then I realized I wasn't going to get very far as the gas gauge was approaching the red line. My mind was racing along with the car. *Where do I go? What do I do?* And if that wasn't enough, red and blue lights flashed in my rearview mirror. I took a squealing turn at the next intersection, slowing down and then revving back up. The road began to swerve one way and then the other. I clenched the wheel with both hands, focusing my gaze. I turned hard to the left, the wheels screamed. I turned back, just in time to stay on the road. The road led up a steep incline, taking me and the car into the pre-morning sky.

Suddenly, the road jutted to the left. I turned. It jutted to the right. I turned back but lost control and skidded onto the gravelly berm. I shoved both feet onto the brake just as the front end collided with the guardrail, stopping the car with a jolting crescendo and throwing open the passenger door. The motor sputtered and went to sleep. I looked to my right. My bags were halfway out the door, money was lying on the seat and spilling out of the car.

The sun was just peeking over the horizon. I stood by the roadside watching the money, earned somewhere in the middle of nowhere, carried over the guardrail and into the valley. My heart sank, yet a strange sense of calm washed over me. The bills continued to flutter like wounded pigeons struggling to stay aflight. Off in the distance, sirens serenaded the coming day. I waited their arrival, strangely relieved that it was almost over.

I turned and looked at the cream-colored Mustang, front smashed into the guardrail, a small trail of smoke rising from the hood. I sat against the rail as the whirring lights became visible down the road. The purring engines revved as they sped toward me with urgency. It was like watching a movie. I felt out of body, as if I were a watcher of some Hollywood feature, part of the crowd who would join in the applause as the villain was handcuffed and thrown in the back of the squad car.

They approached at breakneck speed, throwing gravel in the air as they skidded to a stop a few feet from where I stood. I covered my face with my arms as I was hit with debris. Suddenly, from behind open doors, a dozen guns pointed in my direction. I put my hands in the air and knelt on the ground. I was bombarded by multiple men, thrust to the ground, face planted in the dirt, wrists secured behind my body. I think they read me my rights, but I couldn't be sure, as everything around me was a muffled blur. The movie, with me the antagonist, was still playing in the foreground.

They lifted me to my feet, half dragged me to a waiting car, and tossed me in the back seat. The door slammed. I sat there in a daze, a feeling of relief washing over me.

Chapter Twenty-Four

I sat in a small cell. It was dimly lit with a bench along the back wall. I was transferred from the back seat of the squad car behind a nondescript white building into the back of a windowless van and then was processed somewhere a long way from where the chase began. Few words were spoken. "Get out—duck your head—come on, let's go." I was fingerprinted. "Relax your hand." Mugshot taken. "Turn to your left." And then I sat in a small cell.

Hours passed—or so I assumed. I became restless. I was glad to have made it off the farm, but this wasn't where I wanted to end up. My initial relief as I sat in the back of the squad car gave way to angst as the dim light in the small cell flickered randomly and I lost all sense of time. I pictured myself on the farm sitting under the canopy of trees listening to the sounds of nature, feeling the warm breeze. I thought about the roaring of the engine as hopped-up cars sped by on the track, and rubbing elbows with and being admired by the upper echelon of society. I started to miss it, no matter how corrupt. But I knew that wasn't my reality as my two selves sat in my mind, quietly contemplating life. Just as my time on the farm came with no foreseeable endpoint, I didn't know how long I would be locked away.

A meal was passed through a small opening in the door. I ate cold beans and some kind of meat and washed it down with a warm cup of water. Another tray appeared through the door, stale bacon and runny eggs. And another warm cup of water.

This routine continued and I almost resigned myself to this fate—cold meals and time alone, where time had no reason or purpose.

The occasional trek to the bathroom down a long corridor was the only thing that broke the monotony. "On your feet. Let's go." And then back to the barren cell.

I struggled—for a while. I didn't know how long I had been there—four or five days—a week. But I began to struggle—and it took a few days for me to find ways to keep my sanity. I did push-ups. I did more push-ups. I held my breath and counted and then tried to hold it longer the next time. I did squats in place and then lunges from one end of the cell to the other—which amounted to five each way. I tried meditation. I visualized myself fighting. I visualized myself wrestling. I visualized not knowing if I would ever do those things again—but I visualized again and again. It wasn't as much the isolation, but the not knowing. I didn't know how long I would be there or how long I'd been. So I continued my push-ups, holding my breath, squats and lunges, and living through my own memories.

I was expecting a meal soon. Breakfast, lunch, dinner, it didn't matter, I just needed something to do. I needed my idle hands to be put to use, even if just for a moment. But instead, the door opened wide and a lady in a dark gray pantsuit walked in with a folding chair and sat in front of me.

She crossed her legs, set a manila folder on her lap, and lifted her chin in thought. "My name is Agent Flores." She paused.

"You've been here for a few days, haven't you?" I nodded my head. "How are you getting along?"

I sat for a moment trying to figure out her angle. My former self moved to the forefront. "Well, that depends," I finally answered.

"Okay. I get your reticence. I'm sure you want to know what's going on." She smiled mechanically. "So, I'll just get down to it. You were caught up with some bad people. A big organization, a lot going on behind the scenes I'm sure you weren't aware of. We've been following them for a few years." She leaned forward and looked at me. "We know how you got involved. We know about your fighting for Oscar Jimenez and then your involvement with the Cortez pipeline.

I shook my head. "Don't even know what that is."

"Cortez is the big man you met at the racetrack. He had a pipeline into a bunch of different operations—drugs, under-ground fighting—auto racing—real estate schemes." I raised my eyebrows and laughed quietly. "You find this funny?"

I took a deep breath. "No. I find it ironic."

"What do you mean, ironic?"

"I knew it—I felt it—long time before I met the guy. And I warned myself. A bit too late, mind you, but I was looking for a way out."

"What did you know?"

"Nothing specific. I just knew I was in with some bad people. I made a huge error getting on the plane and then quickly, once I was stuck on the farm, I knew there had to be layers of bad shit going on."

"Right, that's what we figured out. We know your level of involvement. In fact, we wouldn't have done much if you would have given yourself up, but you ran. So we thought we would use you."

"Yeah, where have I heard that before?"

"I'm sure you've heard it a lot, but this will be to your benefit."

"You mind if I go to the bathroom before you give me another offer I can't refuse?"

She grimaced and shook her head, "Sure," and then stood up and knocked on the door. A man popped his head in. "I need you to take the suspect to the lavatory."

I got up and followed the guard down the hall and into a solitary, dimly lit bathroom. I sat on the cold steel of the basin. *Suspect...* the Agent's words bounced around my head. *What was I a suspect for? They knew my involvement.* This is where my former self, the more rational of the two halves, took hold.

I followed the guard back down the hall after I was done. The cell door was still open. Agent Flores was standing outside, in quiet conversation with a man in a suit who wasn't there before I left to relieve myself. I walked in and decided not to sit. The Agent joined me inside. She looked at me and gestured toward the bench.

"You know I've been here for five days—maybe a week." I stayed on my feet, taking whatever control I could over my situation, hearing the voice of the man in the gray suit strengthen my resolve, *you've got balls.* "And I haven't been given a phone call. I haven't been given a chance to talk to a lawyer."

"You're right," she replied frankly. "And you'll get that opportunity, soon. But we need you to understand something first."

"Wait," my former self took complete control. My current self sat back and smiled in the background. "I have a few questions before we go any further."

"Okay—go ahead."

"First," I paused for effect, trying to establish control over space and time, "has anyone been contacted about my situation—do my parents know where I'm at?"

"Do you want them to know?" I pursed my lips, furrowed my brow, and looked at her. And then, shook my head slowly and smiled. "That's what I thought. You sure didn't seem to care much before."

I took a step forward as my current self perked up in the back of my mind. My former self held up a palm to calm him. "So, you have talked to them," My former self said with a biting confidence. I wanted her to know that I was not a brain-damaged fighter rotting away behind a locked door. I wanted her to look at me as a resource, one she could use to further her investigation of this pipeline as she called it. At the same time, I could feel my current self bouncing in the background, warming up, the tingling once again returning to my fingers. I felt I was in for another battle. While my former self knew this to be a battle of intellect, my current self craved the only battle he knew and waited for the bell to begin the fight. I took an internal breath, bringing my two selves in concert.

"Yes—we've talked to your parents," she looked deep into my eyes, the first time I'd felt any sentiment from her, "and they're worried about you."

She was trying to play to my emotions—and I let her know I wasn't participating, even though a pang of sadness welled in my gut. "Of course they are. And you guys haven't even given me the chance to call them."

"The rules are different here, young man."

"I've noticed."

"This is not just a federal investigation. This is international. It spans at least three countries."

"That doesn't surprise me. I told you I knew I was in with some bad people."

"Right—you did."

"That's why I didn't try to get away, I mean, I didn't resist arrest."

"And that was smart."

"Yeah, I know." We stood their for a moment.

"You ready to take a seat again?"

"Maybe, but I can't talk with you freely without knowing what I'm getting myself into."

"Right, I get it."

"I'm sure you do and I'd love to help. I'd love to get myself out of here—but you're baiting me and I can't dig myself any deeper than I have already."

"Well, the reason you've sat in here for a week is because we don't really need you. We know you were a small player." I shook my head, knowing this was another ploy. "You're not the only one we have locked away in a cell."

"That's good to know, but that doesn't give me any assur-ances. It's always the little guys who take the fall while the big guys escape with a slap on the wrist or are never caught in the first place. And if I were to cooperate and tell you everything I know, this Cortez guy sends his henchmen to shank me in my cell." My former self stood up, trying to calm me down, aware that if I started to talk too much, everything would come gushing out.

And she sat there, just waiting for me to implode, for the details to flow like a waterfall and drown me in its wake. She opened the folder on her lap. She pretended to read something

I'm sure she had already memorized and then looked at me and smiled, not saying a word.

I looked down at my hands. The tingling had subsided, but my nerves were rattled. Her strategy was working. I wanted the water to flow. I wanted to confess everything. I wanted to purge months of addiction, months of living a life I was not happy with. But I held strong.

"Okay—it looks like we've gone as far as we can today." She stood up. "You're going to be transferred to general population and will await trial there."

My current self popped up, suddenly ready to grab her and shake her until she told me what was going on, but my other self was there to keep him under wraps. "So, am I ever going to get that call?"

"You'll get your call soon." She turned and walked out. The door closed behind her with a solitary echo.

* * *

I sat on the bottom bunk of a new cell—bright and open in comparison to the last, but after just a few hours I was missing the privacy I had in the once confining cell I just left. A small barred window at the top of the back wall let a teasing light flow across the cement ceiling while a set of bars at the front let all noise in and out. The two bunks and a metal sink and toilet were open viewing to the general population and the guards as they passed by. The one reprieve was the access to reading material. My cellmate informed me that a handful of books were brought by once or twice a week. Luckily he let me read the book he had already read a half dozen times and I lost myself in a Midwest town, clad in denim, a worn wide-brimmed hat, and cowhide boots.

I shuffled in and out of meals and time in the yard. I was compelled to use the rudimentary workout equipment that was sitting in the middle of the cement playground surrounded by a thirty-foot tall chain link fence, barbed wire, and intermittent guard towers, but I thought better of it as I didn't want to draw attention to myself.

The lights went out on the third day as I had just walked into a saloon and sat down to a game of Faro. I made sure to have my back to the wall and my gun at the ready as I knew the Cowboys were on the prowl that night. And then it went dark, I set the book on my chest, and I was left in my own thoughts. Each night since I had been locked up, my thoughts were a mess. They leapt from my current situation to my family—from the farm to the dazzling lights and the golf claps of the marbled, underground, casino-fight club—I saw John and Q riding up front, driving me to one of my first fights in a warehouse in an unknown destination. And then I woke to a dim light floating across the ceiling.

I stood in my cell, did a few squats, jumped in place a few times, and then did a few push-ups. "What the fuck man?" a tired voice came from the top bunk. "Ain't even roll call yet." A pillow flew down and hit me in the back.

I sat on the edge of my bed, wondering what to do next. Almost two weeks in and the unknown time was gnawing at me. A few minutes later, the bars rattled open and we formed a line on the walkway outside our cells. The guard ran through the morning routine. Everyone was accounted for and we marched in unison, forward and then down a set of stairs to the chow line.

As I was finishing up what was supposed to be oatmeal and

toast, a guard informed me that I had a visitor. I scowled, knowing this was not normal at this time of morning, and then followed the guard through a set of barred gates and into a small room. I sat down, the guard handcuffed me to the table, and walked out.

A few minutes later, the door opened and Agent Flores stepped inside. She stood for a moment and then sat down. "So, how've you been?" she asked, adding an awkward smile in an attempt to show a semblance of humanity. I took a breath and looked at her. "You finding your way around alright?"

My current self stood up in haste. *Are you kidding me? He* wanted to yell. But my former self stood up and stepped forward. "Well, I still haven't gotten that phone call," my former self replied.

"Yeah—I know. We're working with something delicate here, and we can't be one hundred percent sure how safe it is for you to make a call."

"Hmmm... not sure if that's your fault or mine, but I'm assuming you're contributing that to me."

"Not really. It's just complicated." She opened what looked to be the same folder from our initial meeting. "You're quite an interesting person. You don't give an inch, do you?"

"Only when it looks like the right move."

"And you don't think it's the right move here?"

"Honestly, I don't know what the right move is, but you haven't given me any clear indication what's going on, so I figure I have to keep everything I got to myself."

"Well, maybe I can help clear things up for you. Just a moment." She opened the door and called to someone in the hall. Another woman, looking much like Agent Flores, in a pantsuit, with shoulder-length dark hair, walked in passed her and stood on the other side of the table from me.

I shook my head. "Shit—okay—you got me," I said between sarcastic laughs.

"So, you recognize Agent Carlisle? "

"I believe so, although she's wearing a bit more clothes than the last time we met." Agent Carlisle smiled. "Where's your other half?" I inquired.

"You mean, Agent Preston? He's nearby," Agent Carlisle assured me.

"So, he's not a manager looking to take me legit?"

"Well, you may be surprised. He actually loves MMA and has some contacts. That's how he landed this case." She smiled. "Anyway, I'm here to clear things up. We're not here for you. We're here for Cortez and his cartel. We know how you got caught up with them. If you cooperate, your record will be wiped clean."

I looked at her for a moment and then closed my eyes. I opened them again, "So, what is it you need from me?"

"Just identify a few key players from some video and photos and tell us any details you know."

"How do I know I'll be safe if you let me go?"

"How do you know you'll be safe in here?" she replied.

* * *

I was sitting in front of a group of six agents. A video camera sat in the corner of the room, pointed at my seat. It had been a week since I last met Agents Flores and Carlisle. This time they brought "the manager of fighters." He was leading the charge—making sure the camera was set correctly, going over questions with his colleagues, and talking to a stenographer who sat near the camera. He settled into a chair across the table and looked at me pleasantly.

"Are you ready?" he asked.

I tried to stay strong—to keep my wits about me—but he had a way of making me feel comfortable. After a few weeks locked up behind bars, I was ready for it to be over.

"It's okay," he smiled. "Take a drink of water before we begin."

I picked up the glass of water in front of me and gulped three times. I set it down and took a few quiet breaths.

"I'm ready."

Agent Preston turned and nodded to the man behind the camera. He read through a prepared document—the date, the time, the location. He introduced himself and then said my name and spelled it for the recording. He ran through the procedure, the types of questions he would be asking, and then outlined the deal we had made if I were to fully cooperate. I was given the opportunity to meet with a lawyer and to talk to my parents briefly before I decided whether to answer their questions.

My parents were distraught, but relieved to hear my voice. They didn't question me, just like when I would come home with a black eye or a bloody lip from the games on the field behind the apartments. They just told me they loved me and were glad I was okay.

An hour later, we were wrapping up. Agent Preston looked me straight in the eye. "Thanks. We appreciate your cooperation." He turned his head and nodded at the cameraman and the recording ended. "It will take three or four days to get the paperwork in order and then I'll personally come back and escort you home."

CHAPTER TWENTY-FOUR

"Thanks." I stood and shook his hand. "I appreciate it."

"You're a brave soul, young man." He nodded and walked out.

Agents Flores and Carlisle walked over and shook my hand. Everyone filed out, and I was left alone.

A feeling of relief overtook me, and I felt tears welling in my eyes.

Chapter Twenty-Five

I found myself in a small hotel room next door to Agent Preston. The last two months had been a whirlwind. He did as he said he would, first of all, meeting me at the detention center and escorting me home after a long three-day wait. I spent a full two weeks at home, reuniting with my parents and recovering from the ordeal. I did briefly connect with John and Q. They were in their normal stupor, but worked their way out of it just enough to get a semblance of what I had gone through, I think. And then, Agent Preston fulfilled his first promise, the one he revealed while he and Agent Carlisle met me in my dressing room as undercover fight manager and "partner," to take me legit.

We were in a hotel waiting to meet with a fight team the next day. He used his time undercover to scout talent and presented my story to his friend who trains and manages a number of MMA fighters—a few who have fought around the world, and one who was currently ranked in the UFC. He told me that if my workout went well, I could walk away with a signed contract.

The next day, I woke to a drizzly, gray morning. It was early, so I threw on sweats, pulled my hood tight over my head, and decided to go for a run. I popped my earbuds in and let the music carry me away, while I made my way onto the pavement and let my legs take me from a walk to a slow jog.

It felt good to finally be in control of my life again. I didn't know the exact direction I was headed yet, but I had a feeling good things were underfoot. I ran down the sidewalk and watched as the city began to wake up. Ever since I'd been locked up, I seemed to notice the little details around me at a more heightened level—the enticing aroma as I passed a corner coffee shop—fresh bread as patrons walked in and out of a small cafe—and the oddly comforting sounds of traffic as it made its way up and down the street.

By the time I was back at the hotel and showered, Agent Preston was ready to head out. I grabbed a Glacier White VitaWater from the mini fridge and a couple of protein bars, staples of my training, and was ready for a day of hard work. I hadn't worked out with anyone for nine months, since I was back in college, and I was looking forward to it. It was hard to believe it had been nine months since I left my college wrestling room and three months since I stole the cream-colored Mustang and fled the farm. I couldn't believe what my life had become in such a short time and was determined to make the best of this opportunity.

We arrived at an industrial park and wound our way through a few buildings until we came to a warehouse near the back. There were two cars parked in front. The large garage door was up and a hip-hop rhythm greeted us as we stepped out of the car. We grabbed our bags out of the trunk, and the driver turned the car around and drove off. We walked inside, a lone figure was near the back, just visible behind a cage that sat in the middle of the room. A rhythmic woosh-whoosh-whoosh-whoosh filled the back corner as the figure gracefully jumped rope and kept time with the music.

Agent Preston, who I now called Terry, led me to a small office at the front of the gym.

"Holy shit, you made it." A middle-aged man with a crooked nose and a lifetime of fighting on his face walked out from behind a desk full of papers with open arms.

"Hey, Jeremy, it's been a while," Terry replied joyfully. They embraced. "This place looks nice, much better than the garage you were at a few years ago."

"That dump. Don't want to think about that place. We don't have to worry about mopping rain off the mats here," he laughed.

"Yeah—I remember that."

They spent a couple minutes catching up and then Terry introduced me.

"This is the fighter I was telling you about," he stepped aside and brought his open palm in front of me.

"Terry's told me your story," Jeremy confirmed. I stepped forward and shook his hand. He looked me up and down. "Sounds like you've had some interesting experiences."

"You can say that," I smiled.

"You up for a workout today? I've got a fighter here who's gonna show you around and take you through a warm up before we do any contact. She's tough, one of our better prospects. And then I have a couple guys around your size who should be showing up in the next hour. You can roll around with them and we can see what you got. Sound good?"

"Yeah, I'm up for anything."

"Just like Terry said," he smiled and shook his head.

He took us to the back of the gym and introduced us to the fighter jumping rope. "Hey, Kimmy," he motioned to the figure jumping rope.

200

She stopped jumping, reached up, and pulled her hood off her head. She was breathing heavily. Sweat was dripping from her forehead. "Hey, Coach," she said between breaths.

"This is my friend Terry and the fighter you'll be warming up." He introduced us. "Do your best to tire him out. You have an hour before the other guys show up." And then he and Terry disappeared into the office.

She bent down, picked up a small towel from a chair against the wall, and wiped the sweat from her forehead. "So, Coach was telling me you done quite a bit of fighting."

"Yeah. I've had quite a few fights."

"What's your discipline?"

"I'm a wrestler."

"Can you take a punch?"

"Yeah, I can take a punch. And I can give a pretty good one, too." I tilted my head and smiled.

"Well, I guess we'll see about that." She pulled her hood back over her head. "Follow me, I'll show you the locker room. You can change and then I'll take you around the gym."

When I came back out, Kimmy had taken off her sweats and was wearing black tights just below her knees and a red sports bra. She had a dragon tattoo on the left side of her torso and a series of images and words tattooed on her left arm.

"Let's start over here." She took me to the back corner and we did a full loop around the gym, ending up in an area with cardio and weight equipment. "So—I'm supposed to get you warmed up. Where do you want to begin?"

I looked around. "I'd like to get a sweat going on the treadmill and then do some movement drills. To be honest, I'd like to do a bit of everything. I haven't been in the gym as much as I would have liked the past couple months."

"Okay, how bout you start on the treadmill and then show me your movement drills? And since you said you can punch, I'll take you through a couple mitt routines."

Fifteen minutes later we were in the middle of the cage. I walked several times around and then skipped, hopped, and jogged.

"So, I usually do a bit of a wrestling warm-up," I turned to Kimmy who had been jogging slowly around the cage.

"Okay, show me what you got."

I spent the next few minutes moving in a stance and shadow-wrestling. And then popped up and threw jabs into the air.

"Okay big guy, looks like you can throw, but you're a bit off balance," she chided. "Let's go through a couple mitt routines and clean that up."

"Truthfully, I learned how to punch in the ring—kind of a do-or-die thing—and I've just hit the bags—never used mitts."

"You'll catch on quickly. I can tell."

She worked me through three simple combinations and then stepped back, "You got that pretty easily. Let's change it up. One-Two-Three-Two and then step under to your right." She demonstrated the added steps in slow motion and then held the mitts in front of me.

Bam—Bam—Bam—Bam—Duck—Step.

Bam—Bam—Bam—Bam—Duck—Step.

She added a few more wrinkles... shuffling away to the right—and then shuffling back to the left and throwing jabs. By the end, I was moving quickly and with confidence.

Bam-Bam-Bam-Bam-Duck-Step-Shuffle-Bam-Bam-Bam.

Bam-Bam-Bam-Bam-Duck-Step-Shuffle-Bam-Bam-Bam.

"Well," she shrugged, 'you got that, too. I'm impressed."

"It's fun," I said, catching my breath.

"I think you're ready for more than I can give you," she smiled.

"Not sure about that. I bet you've got quite a bit more." I smiled back and felt a little tingling in my body, but this time the tingling was for another reason altogether. We looked at each other awkwardly. I wasn't used to flirting and I could tell I caught her off guard, but she didn't back down.

"Yeah, I've got a few tricks up my sleeve."

"Maybe you can show them to me sometime."

She shook her head, "Not sure you could handle it," throwing back like a true fighter.

We sat down and leaned against the cage.

"So, how long you been fighting?" I asked.

"About three years. Coach found me working out at a boxing club not far from here. I didn't know what I was doing."

"You seem to know what you're doing now."

"He's helped me a lot. What about you? When'd you start fighting?"

"Really, about nine months ago."

"Shit—nine months? I wouldn't have guessed."

"Well, it's not that simple."

Just then, Jeremy's voice boomed over a loudspeaker, "Kimmy, the guys are here, bring him out and introduce him."

We got out of the cage. There were two young fighters standing next to Jeremy's office. We walked over and shook hands. Jeremy told the two guys to warm-up and get ready for sparring. And twenty minutes later I was back in the cage.

"Grappling only for the first round," Jeremy told us. I raised my hand in agreement and in less than a minute had my partner down and in control. I let him up and stood in front of him and allowed him to shoot on my legs. I stood my ground as he tried to take me down and then shuffled away and out of his grasp. We both stood up. I walked forward and into a clinch. We moved around, jockeying for position. I lowered my level, ducked under his arm, swooshed behind him, and lifted him off his feet and to the ground. The round ended.

"Okay, guys—put on headgear for the second round and stay on your feet. Remember, this is sparring. Keep it clean."

I could tell my partner was more comfortable on his feet. He bobbed and moved, and then stepped toward me as the round began. I circled and watched him for a moment. He stepped in and through a combination. I stood in front of him and blocked his punches with my raised fists. He threw another combination. I stepped to the side and threw a jab, catching him on the side of the head. The round continued. I moved, jabbed, landed punches with ease. He started getting frustrated and backed off. I backed off and gave him a chance to catch his breath and the round ended.

"You ready for another challenger?" Jeremy yelled through the chain link.

I nodded and my next partner, a bit taller than me, with long, lanky arms, stepped into the octagon. We followed the same procedures—a round of grappling and a round on our feet. He had better defense on the ground when I took him down and had quicker hands. He managed to catch me with one punch, which slid off the side of my face without much impact. I landed three or four good combinations before the end of the second round.

Kimmy hopped into the ring and helped me take off my headgear. She smiled without saying a word and then quickly slapped me in the face with her right hand. "Luckily you didn't have to face me." She sauntered off and then shot me a glare over her shoulder as she walked out of the ring. I felt my already beating heart speed up.

After the workout was over, we all sat on the mats in front of the ring. "So, Terry was right. You have talent. Jordy and Raul here are good fighters." He looked at them, "No offense boys, but he made you look like beginners." He turned back to me. "And I'm not just saying that. They're good, they've won lots of fights against good fighters, but you are just on another level." He turned to Terry, "You ready to do some business?"

"I am—but you gotta ask my fighter," he turned to me and winked.

"You ready?" Jeremy asked me.

"I'm ready," I said with confidence, nodding my head.

"Okay—shower up and meet in the office, don't want you dripping sweat on the contract," he scoffed.

I got up and headed to the locker room.

"Hey," Kimmy called my name. I turned around. "I've gotta get home soon." She paused. "You gonna be hanging around here now?"

"I hope so."

"Good—I'll challenge you to a match next time."

I watched as she smiled over her shoulder and disappeared into the locker room.

* * *

Terry was sitting on the couch on the far side of the office sipping on a bottled water. Jeremy was standing by his desk, a pair of black-rimmed glasses low on his nose, reading a document with his chin held high.

"Okay, looks like everything's here." He sat down next to

Terry on the couch and put the document on the coffee table in front of him. I sat down across the table and we went over the contract in detail. I asked a few questions and we discussed a few options regarding fight promotions and competitions. He told me we'd start with a few local events to get my name out. "They will all be well-respected fighters," he said, "but most likely nothing at the level you're used to."

"When do you think I'll get to move up to something big?" The tingling in my fingers began to appear. I opened and closed my hands several times trying to keep it under control.

"Well, that depends on what you mean by big. If you mean the UFC, that's probably a couple years away, if it's even possible. From everything I've seen and from what Terry has told me, I think you have the talent, but it's about more than just talent. It's about finding the right path. It's about contacts—about who you know."

I shook my head and leaned back in my chair.

Terry looked at me and sat forward. "I know you're used to tough fighters and high-stakes matches. Remember, I've been there. I've seen you fight. That's why I brought you here. But, you've also got to remember, nobody knows you yet. You can't use those fights on your resume. It will take a bit of time to build your professional record and your reputation. I have faith in what Jeremy can do for you, but you have to feel comfortable with the situation. We're not going to force you into anything you don't want to do."

I sat quietly.

"One thing I can promise you," Jeremy said, looking at me intently, "I'll do everything I can to get you into one of the big fight promotions. It may take a few months, maybe even a year, to get you started with one of the smaller ones to start with, but

I have no doubt, if you work hard, you will find yourself moving up quickly."

I rubbed my face with my palms. The tingling continued faintly at the tips of my fingers. I took a deep breath to control my urges. I looked at him. "Well, that sounds good."

"I've got one more angle I'll be working on while we get you started. I know someone who is involved with the Professional Fighters League and I called him up after Terry initially contacted me."

"Wow—you mean the PFL?"

"Yeah, but there isn't an opening right now. I did get you on the alternates list, though."

"Oh—what's an alternate do?"

"You fill in if one of the fighters drops out for some reason. I can't promise anything. In fact, I don't know how many alternates they have. But at least your name is there. If you don't make it in this time, you have a shot at getting in the next season—in a few months— if things go well. For now, we just need to get some fights under your belt."

Chapter Twenty-Six

Pop-pop—pop-pop. Dance—bounce-bounce. Pop-pop—pop-pop. Dance—bounce-bounce. It was the second of my two-a-day workouts. I was training for my official pro-debut just one month after I signed my contract with Coach Terry. It was seven p.m. I was pushing through a circuit, pounding away at the heavy bag.

"Time," Coach Terry's voice rang out. "Into the cage."

I ran two laps around the cage, then hopped up the stairs and through the open gate. A twelve-minute grapple match with two sparring partners tagging in every three minutes.

"Three... two... one..." Coach yelled, and then blew the whistle.

I met my first partner in the middle of the ring. This was full go—no dancing or feeling each other out. We collided. I lowered my level, wrapped my arms around his legs, lifted him, and drove him against the chain link. He found his footing and fended off the takedown. Just as he broke free from my grip I dropped my level again and took him straight to the ground. He found his guard and we fought for control. I was able to slip his guard and gain a side mount. I'd been working on my submissions the last two weeks, but my partner was adept at defending and was able to slip holds and evade my locks.

"Time," Coach bellowed.

As I stood up, my next partner was on top of me, grabbing me from behind. He started to take me to the ground, but I broke his lock and got free. The match continued at a high pace until the twelve minutes were up.

I hopped down the stairs, ran two laps around the cage, and bounded back up and in. My trainer slipped my headgear on my head and my mouthpiece in my mouth. I had four, two-minute sparring matches. The same two partners switched in every two minutes with a one-minute rest in between.

THWAP—THWAP—I landed blows—bobbed, moved, and blocked a combination with my raised hands. THWAP—THWAP—I landed two more punches and continued moving. When time was up I ran two laps around the cage and jumped on the treadmill. I ran intervals for ten minutes and jogged for five.

I finished with the speed bag, push-ups, and medicine ball sit-ups. When I was done, I jogged to the center of the cage and lay on my back—my favorite part of the workout—feeling my heart recover, as sweat dripped from my body and pooled on the canvas.

When I was done, I sat up. Kimmy was leaning on the cage with a playful smile. "You sure you're up for tonight?" she teased.

"Of course. Just give me a few minutes to shower up."

"Reservations are at eight-thirty."

"I know—I won't be long."

"You better not be. You don't want to miss your last full meal."

"Don't remind me," I groaned, half-heartedly. I got to my knees and took a deep breath, and then walked out of the cage and wrapped my sweaty arms around her.

"Okay, that's enough. This is the only nice outfit I got." She ducked out of my embrace with a little shove. "Get your ass in the shower so we can go."

"Alright—alright," I surrendered, raising my hands above my head. "I'll get cleaned up."

Half an hour later, as we headed out the door, Coach Terry was standing outside his office, a mischievous smile on his face.

"Where you guys headed?" he called playfully.

"A night on the town," Kimmy grinned. "I'm taking him out for his final meal before he begins starving himself tomorrow."

"Oh yeah? Better fill that belly," he joked, flashing a grin before disappearing back into his office.

We made it to the restaurant just in time for our reservation. It was nothing fancy, but all I cared about was shoveling as many calories into my body as I could and soaking up as much time with Kimmy as possible. Ever since we met that first day at the gym, I was hooked. And soon we were meeting there almost every day.

After dinner, I walked her back to her place. She lived up two flights of stairs in a small studio apartment. I held her hand as she led me up to the top floor. We slowed down as we approached her door and stood there for a moment.

"You wanna come in for a while?" she finally asked.

I looked down at my feet and leaned forward, placing my forehead on hers. "You know I do," taking a deep breath, "but it's getting late. I've gotta stay focused."

"I know," she said breathlessly.

"I promise. We'll spend more time outside the gym after my fight."

"I'm gonna hold you to it."

"You won't have to. I just hope you don't get sick of me by then. The fights still a week away."

"Yeah—true. You'll have to be on your best behavior."

I gave her a soft kiss on the lips and looked into her eyes, "My best behavior," I stated with confidence.

I took a step back. She held tight to my hand as our arms stretched apart. We stood and looked at each other.

She tilted her head. "See you at the gym."

"Yep—bright and early." I let go of her hand and jogged down the stairs.

* * *

It was nine a.m. I stripped down to my boxers and stepped onto the scale. The ref raised his hand and certified my weight. My opponent stepped on and off the scale, and then we faced off in front of a small crowd. Flashes went off as local papers documented the affair. Three other fights were scheduled on the card, with mine set for second to last. After everything I had been through, I was fighting in the undercard of a local event—well, not totally local. My opponent was actually from Mexico. But I had been through so much it seemed like small stakes, though Coach Terry assured me that a couple of these fights and things would move quickly.

The next day, the bout was over almost before it began. The bell rang and we were on our feet for less than a minute. He swung a wild combination. I ducked under his flailing arms and took him to the canvas. I proceeded to pound his face. The ref jumped in between us and pushed me to the side. It was a relief—actual rules—with stoppages. It allowed me to fight freely. I didn't have to worry about anything but fighting.

Two more fights with much the same outcome—one ground and pound and a second, three combinations and a right hook sent my opponent face first into the canvas. My work with an actual trainer was paying off. My handwork, both on my feet and on the mat, was measurably better and I was even learning some simple low and mid-level kicks.

Three months after I joined my new team, I got big news. Coach Terry knew that all the fights he could get me with local promoters were way below my level, so he had been pulling out all the stops and calling in every favor he was owed. Up until now, though, he wasn't having any luck. But, as I relaxed with Kimmy on a crash pad after our morning workout, Coach Terry walked up and handed me his laptop. "Read the first paragraph," he said with a crooked smile.

I read—and then jumped up—"Holy shit."

"Hold on, don't break my laptop," he laughed and reached over and grabbed it from my hands as I jumped in circles.

"Is this real?" I yelled with surprise.

"You bet your ass it's real."

"Hold on, what are you guys talking about?" Kimmy stood up and looked from me to Coach.

"I'm invited to the PFL Challenger Series."

"What? Oh my god." Kimmy jumped into my arms. "What happened? I thought you said it was full?"

"Yeah—it was," I bellowed as I squeezed her tight, "but somebody got injured and they want me to fill in."

"When do you need to leave?" Kimmy asked.

I turned to Coach.

"Probably tomorrow," he said, rubbing the top of his head. He took a deep breath and let it out. "Your first fight is in three days and then we'll figure out the rest of the tournament when we get back."

Kelly and I danced around, embraced, and fell into the crash pad. I turned onto my side and looked at her. "You going to be okay without me?"

She smiled and nodded, "The question is, are you going to be okay without me?"

We laughed and then lay in each other's arms for the next thirty minutes, talking about the whirlwind of circumstances that brought us to this moment and letting our sweaty bodies cool down. We talked about the fight. We dreamed about what we were going to do when I came back in four months with the belt and prize money. We talked about our future. We talked about the fact that neither of us had been in a long-term relationship before and didn't really know what to do.

And then I sat up, feeling a sudden sense of urgency. "I'm not sure what's going to happen, but I'm going to approach this the same way I approach all my fights. I expect to win. I've always trained to win."

She looked up at me and smiled and we sat there for a moment.

"The difference is," I added, "I want you to be here when I return."

She pulled me on top of her, "I don't plan on going any-where."

Chapter Twenty-Seven

It was early morning. I was covered in sweat gear pedaling away on a stationary bike, working the last half pound off before weigh-in. My first fight of the tournament was just over twenty-four hours away. My next fight would be in a month. After the two preliminary fights, the top four fighters from each weight class would move on to the semi-finals. Each step takes place thirty days after the previous step, with the finals taking place four months from the start of the tournament. It was a totally different world, from an almost no holds barred fight, sometimes multiple fights a night, to sanctioned matches spaced out with enough time to train and fully recover before stepping back in the cage.

The next evening, my hand was raised after a knockout in the first round. I was amazed how effective my striking had become since working with Jeremy and his team. Thirty days later, I ended my second preliminary fight with a quick takedown and a barrage of punches. In the semi-finals, I was matched up against a rangy submission specialist. He wasn't much on his feet, but submitted both of his previous opponents with an ankle lock and an armbar toward the end of the third round. I wasn't overly impressed, though. I knew I had fought a number of tougher guys in my previous life. So I was confident as I hopped into the cage and heard the announcer's voice boom over the crowd.

When the fight began, he was hunched over with his hands in front of his face. I had a difficult time getting through his defense. I didn't land any meaningful punches in the first round and couldn't get to his legs effectively. I had him against the fence a couple times, and kneed him twice, but that was about it.

The second round began and I pushed the pace. I wanted to get him winded and take him to the ground before the round ended. I was still using my two selves to balance my life, so I used them to maintain focus but remained aggressive. By this time, my two selves had pretty much melded into one, and I had learned to use them together effectively. I was learning to call upon my own calm when needed and my own Little Demon when necessary.

He stumbled just a bit, trying to evade one of my punches. I could tell his legs were heavy. I lowered my level and shot. He fell to his butt before he could regain his balance. I climbed to a full mount and let my fists fly. With just seconds left in the second round, the fight was over.

Not long after, I was watching my next opponent end his fight with ease—falling off to the side and catching an armbar for a quick tap out. I could tell he was at a much higher level than my first three opponents. He had a more extensive background, a lot of experience on his feet and with submissions.

* * *

The final was just minutes away. I hopped up and down. I crouched down and ran through my usual wrestler's warm-up.

I stood up and threw punches in the air. Jeremy was there beside me. My parents, Kimmy, and Terry were in the crowd, waiting for me to enter the arena.

The door opened and Jeremy led me out. I walked toward the cage for the championship bout and was transferred back in time. I was suddenly making my way through a maze of dinner tables in the marbled room, under a maze of hallways, in a nameless mansion. I heard the roulette tables clicking on the side, the clinking of silverware and glasses. As I stepped onto the stairs, Billy was standing in the middle of the octagon announcing my entrance, "Who's man enough to take on The Little Demon?" he belted. I stepped onto the worn grass where I had played hundreds of kickball and football games, and graduated from the many grass-stained matches on the field behind the apartments. I looked around and saw Chan with a smile on his face, sitting and watching, as if still nine years old, surrounded by a horde of prepubescent boys hooping and hollering, loose change in hand. Billy called us to the center, told us to fight fair, then separated us before the fight began.

I bounced on my side of the grassy ring and waited. The sun beamed down from above. My heart pounded and my fingers tingled, my two selves joined as one, ready for the bell to beckon me forward.

* * *

Two weeks later, we walked along the sidewalk that led us back to the two-story building where Kimmy lived ever since Jeremy invited her to train at his gym three years ago. We had spent the day together, celebrating my return and her submission against a top-level fighter two nights ago. It was overcast, a light mist in the air. I put my hand around her shoulders and pulled her close. We walked silently, enjoying the night.

When we reached her building, I let go of her and she took my hand. She led me up the two flights of stairs to her studio apartment and we paused in front of the door. She searched for her keys among the cluttered contents of her purse and then turned around and threw her arms around my neck, keys jingling in her hand.

She tilted her head, "Do I have to ask?"

I closed my eyes and took a soft breath, a smile radiating on my face.

She turned back, unlocked the door, and I followed her inside.